THE CHANEY EDGE

Chaney Brothers 2

ROBERT VAUGHAN

WOLFPACK
PUBLISHING
— EST 2013 —

WOLFPACK PUBLISHING
— EST 2013 —

Paperback Edition
Copyright © 2019 Robert Vaughan

Published in the United States by Wolfpack Publishing, Las Vegas

Wolfpack Publishing
6032 Wheat Penny Avenue
Las Vegas, NV 89122

wolfpackpublishing.com

Paperback ISBN 978-1-64119-746-5
eBook ISBN 978-1-62918-938-3

Library of Congress Control Number: 2019947842

THE CHANEY EDGE

CHAPTER 1

BUCK CHANEY WAS ASLEEP, AND IN HIS dream he was back on the family farm in southeast Missouri, plowing a field. He was walking behind a mule, watching the dirt fold away from the plowshare as it opened a deep, new furrow. A few yards in front of him his brother, Lance, was plowing another furrow, while a few yards in front of his brother, their father was breaking open a row. Half the field had already been tilled and the coal-black dirt glistened with the nutrients that made the soil so fertile.

Buck's sister, Becky, was standing at the edge of the field, carrying a bucket of water and holding the dipper out toward her father and two brothers. Water was spilling from the dipper, and in the sunlight the water glistened; first silver, then gold, then scarlet. The water became redder and redder still, and it cascaded from the dipper in torrents, rushing across the ground and turning the black dirt red. Then the water became blood and when Buck looked back at Becky he saw that the blood wasn't coming from the dipper; it was coming from several wounds on her body. Buck dropped the reins and tried to run toward his sister, but no matter how hard he willed his legs to work, he couldn't make them move fast enough. Becky was dying before his very eyes and there was nothing he could do to stop it. He cried out in despair.

"Are you all right? Sir? Sir, are you all right?" When Buck opened his eyes he found that he was looking into the face of a very pretty young woman. She was standing in the aisle of the car, leaning down over him, her eyes shining gold in the light of the kerosene lantern which was mounted, nearby, on the wall. He realized then that he wasn't back in southeast Missouri; he was riding on a train in west Texas. He could feel the gentle swaying of the car as it clipped along the track at over twenty miles per hour. Self-consciously, Buck sat up straight in his seat, then ran his hand through blond hair which he kept cut, trail-long.

"Uh, I'm sorry," Buck mumbled. "What did you ask me?"

"You cried out in your sleep," the woman explained. "I'm sure you were having a bad dream."

"Yes," Buck said. "I must've been."

Well awake now, and with the grogginess passed, he was able to more fully examine the young woman who had come to his rescue. She was young, perhaps in her early twenties, and with a fresh-scrubbed look of innocence about her. Buck was about to invite her to join him, when a man's voice called out to her.

"Becky? Becky, you mustn't bother the gentleman any further." The speaker was an army lieutenant.

"Yes, dear," Becky replied. She smiled brightly at Buck. "That's my husband, Lieutenant Billy Murchison. He just graduated from West Point last month and we were married the very next day. Now, we're going to his first assignment."

"As an officer, I should be addressed as William, dear, not Billy," the young lieutenant corrected. "And anyway, I'm sure the gentleman isn't concerned about our history or our destination."

"Nonsense," Buck replied. "I wish you all the luck in the world. After all, I was a lieutenant too, once."

"In the war?" Murchison asked, instantly curious.

"Yes," Buck said. He chuckled, and pointed at the young officer's blue uniform. "Though I'm afraid the uniform I wore wasn't that color."

"Oh, my!" the young woman gasped. "You mean you were a Rebel?"

"Yes," Buck said. "But my brother was a Yankee Captain so I reckon the family honor was spared, even if I did stray."

"At West Point they told us that the war sometimes pitted brother against brother," the young lieutenant said. "That was the real tragedy. Have you and your brother reconciled your differences?"

"Reconciled?" Buck replied with a chuckle. "Yes, that's a good word for it. I guess you could say we have reconciled. He lives his life and I live mine, but you might even say we are friends now."

"And what about the rest of your family?" Becky asked. "How do they feel?"

Buck cleared his throat and stroked his chin. "Well, I'm afraid there is no rest of the family," he said. "They all died, during the war."

"Oh, I'm so sorry," Becky said, her eyes misting over instantly. "Please forgive me for bringing up an unpleasant memory."

"You didn't bring it up, Miss," Buck said. "Such memories are never too far away."

In fact, the memory was no further away than the dream Buck had just had. The dream was a recurring one, though, fortunately, he didn't have it too often. Whenever he did have it, however, it reminded him of his own responsibility for his sister's death. As an officer in a band of Confederate guerrillas, Buck had led his men to his family home in order to avoid capture by Union soldiers. Later, some of those same men returned to the house where they raped and killed his sister.

Though Buck had never completely gotten over it, it had been a long time since he had had such a dream, and at first he wondered what caused the dream to come back. Then, when he heard the young lieutenant address his wife as "Becky," he realized that he must have heard the name while he was still sleeping, and, somehow, that brought on the dream.

After Becky returned to her husband, Buck settled back in the seat, pulled his hat back over his eyes and, soon, was asleep once more. This time it was, mercifully, without dreams.

It was about an hour later when the train suddenly ground to a shuddering, screeching, banging, halt. Buck woke with a start and looked through the window in an effort to see what had caused their sudden stop. It was very dark outside and the gimbal-mounted coal-oil lanterns which lit the inside of the car reflected on the glass, thus making it even more difficult to see through the windows.

"Billy, what do you think it is?" Becky asked. "Why did we stop so abruptly?"

"I don't have any idea," Billy said, straining to look through the window. "I can't see a thing out there."

Though he was having no more success at seeing through the window than Billy, Buck suddenly got a very strong feeling of what was going on. He pulled his pistol and held it on his lap, covering it with his hat. His feeling was substantiated when, a moment later, an ill-kempt, gruff-looking man suddenly stepped onto the front of the car. The man was brandishing a pistol.

"You folks just stay where you are and no one's goin' to get hurt," he shouted.

"See here! What is this?" one of the passengers shouted indignantly. He started to get up, but the gunman moved quickly toward him and brought his pistol down, sharply, over the man's head. The passenger groaned and fell back. A woman who had been sitting with him cried out in alarm.

"What do you think you're doing?" Billy called, standing up quickly. "You can't come in here like this!"

"Billy, please, don't!" Becky cried out in alarm.

The gunman looked at the young lieutenant, then laughed. "Well, look at the soldier-boy, all decked out in his nice, shiny, new uniform. If you don't want blood all over that pretty blue suit you're wearin', soldier-boy, you better sit back down and listen to the little girl."

"I have no intention of being bullied by you, or by anyone else!" Billy said indignantly.

"Sit down, Lieutenant!" Buck said sharply, and, as if hearing a command from a senior officer, Billy followed Buck's orders.

"Now there's a fella who's got some sense," the gunman said. "All the rest of you, just listen to him and stay in your seats. We'll be gone before you know it."

Another gunman came on board the car to join the first. "What's goin' on in here?" he asked. "Why all the talkin'?"

"Don't worry about it. It ain't nothin' I can't handle. What's happening out there? Has Ruthless got the money yet?"

"What are you doin', spoutin' his name all over the place? Are you crazy?"

"I'm sorry."

"Yeah? If he had heard that you'd be more than sorry, you'd be dead. You better learn to keep your mouth shut."

"I reckon you're right," the first gunman said. "Just hurry it up, will you?"

"You stay in here and keep ever'one in their seats 'til we're ready to get out of here."

"How will I know when you're ready? I mean, you won't leave me, will you?"

"We ain't goin' to leave you. We'll blow the whistle before we go. You keep 'em quiet in here, and I'll see what's goin' on in the next car."

As the second gunman started down the aisle to go to the next car, he looked over toward Buck and saw that Buck was holding a pistol under his hat.

"Hey, Pinkus! Look out! This here fella has a gun!" he called, bringing his gun around toward Buck.

Buck hadn't really intended to use the gun. He had only pulled it as a precautionary measure. Now that he was seen, however, he had no choice. It was either shoot, or be shot. Buck shot first, his bullet blasting a hole through the top of his own hat, then plunging into the gunman's chest. The gunman went down.

Pinkus managed to get off a shot but he was too excited and he hurried his shot. His bullet crashed, without effect, through the window. Buck brought his own pistol around and squeezed off a second shot, and Pinkus staggered back, his hands to his throat. Blood spilled through his fingers and he pulled his hands away and stared at them, stupidly, as he went down.

Becky had screamed when the first shot was fired, but now she, like the others, sat mesmerized by the sudden and unexpected turn of events. Everyone else had sat quietly, as instructed. Only Buck managed to react, and, as the car filled with the gun smoke of the three discharges, he scooted out through the back door of the car, jumped from

THE CHANEY EDGE | 9

the steps down to the ground, then fell and rolled out into the darkness.

"Pinkus! Marty! What's goin' on in there?" someone called. "What's all the shootin'?"

In the dim light that spilled through the car windows, Buck could see the gunman who was yelling at the others. One of the two men inside had referred to him as Ruthless. Buck had seen wanted posters on Ruthless Blanton, and though he couldn't see this man very well, he fit the general description according to size. The last poster Buck saw had offered a one-thousand-dollar reward for Ruthless's capture. Buck felt a moment of elation. It was as if the money had just dropped into his lap.

"Hold it right there, Ruthless!" Buck called to the outlaw. "I've got you covered. Put down your gun and throw up your hands."

"What the hell?" Ruthless responded. He realized then that he was in a patch of light, so he moved into the shadow to fire at Buck. Buck had thought he was safe in the darkness, but Ruthless's shot came uncomfortably close, clipping off a small piece of cloth from the shoulder of his shirt. Buck returned fire, using the muzzle blast from Ruthless's own shot as his target. Ruthless had anticipated that, however, and moved as soon as he shot, so Buck's bullet missed. Buck heard the sound of boots scraping on the cinders and he knew that Ruthless was running. Buck snapped off another shot into the darkness and saw his bullet send up sparks as it struck the rocks. He didn't get a third shot at him, because Ruthless disappeared in the night.

"Mister, I don't know who you are!" the train conductor said after it was all over, hopping down from the train to start pumping Buck's hand. "But you just saved the train. Why, do you have any idea who that was you drove away? That was old 'Ruthless' himself. Rufus T. Blanton. Yes, sir that was some shootin' you did."

"It wasn't good enough," Buck said. "He got away."

"He may have gotten away," the conductor said. "But he didn't get what he came for. And, he left two of his friends behind. Yes, sir, the railroad owes you a debt of gratitude."

When Buck climbed back onto the car he saw that the two men he had shot were already being carried away. The conductor told him they were being taken to the baggage car so that "decent folks wouldn't have to put up with their smelling carcasses."

The other passengers in the car, though obviously thankful that he may have saved them, were nevertheless somewhat frightened at being in such close proximity with a man who could so readily and efficiently dispense death. Other than the conductor, no one said a word to him, and though he didn't feel a need to be thanked, he was made uneasy by their fear of him. Becky seemed especially frightened of him, and she buried her face in her husband's arm so she wouldn't even have to look at him.

Lieutenant William Murchison, on the other hand, looked at him with wide-eyed admiration. It was clear that the young lieutenant was awed by what he had just seen and was, perhaps, trying to assess how his own performance might be under similar circumstances. Buck honestly didn't know which made him more uncomfortable, the hero-worship of the new lieutenant, or the fear of the lieutenant's young wife.

As Rufus Blanton rode off into the night, he cursed the stranger who had shot Pinkus and Marty, and, more importantly, had denied him his prize. He didn't know who the passenger was but he figured it wouldn't be too hard to find out. The railroad and all the passengers on the train were calling him a hero, and heroes didn't generally hide their light under a basket. Ruthless decided that he would find out who this "hero" was and then he would kill him.

CHAPTER 2

LANCE CHANEY, DEPUTY MARSHAL OF Barlow, Texas, kept his eyes on the back of the neck of the man who was riding in front of him. His prisoner's name was Titus Lattimore, and two weeks ago Lattimore had killed a bank teller while trying to hold up a bank. There had been no need to shoot the bank teller. The teller had complied with Lattimore's demand to put all the money in the cloth bag he was given. But Lattimore thought that killing the teller would frighten the others in the bank into keeping still long enough for him to make his getaway.

Lattimore was wrong. Instead of frightening the others, it incensed them, and from the moment he set foot outside the front door of the bank they were shouting the alarm. There were two or three armed citizens on the street and they started shooting at Lattimore as he rode away. Lattimore wasn't hit, but, in the commotion of being forced to dodge their bullets while also trying to return fire, he dropped the cloth sack of money he was carrying. This was the same money he had just killed for. As a result of the town's spirited defense, the bank recovered the entire $611, and for all his troubles, Titus Lattimore was left with nothing.

The robbery had actually occurred in a town called Sweetgrass, but when Dan Efrem, the town marshal for Barlow, heard that Lattimore was last seen heading his way, he had a pretty good hunch where Lattimore might be hiding. Actually, it was much more than just a hunch. It was an informed estimate, based upon his years of experience as a lawman, and a thorough knowledge of the country. He also understood the habits of men on the run. Dan told his deputy, Lance Chaney, where he thought Lattimore might be, and Chaney rode out to have a. look.

Lance was not surprised to find that Dan Efrem had been absolutely correct in his analysis. Lance wasn't surprised, but Titus Lattimore was. Lance's arrival in the outlaw's camp was so unexpected that Lattimore had to be awakened from a sound sleep in order to be arrested.

Lance had picked Lattimore up early this morning. It was now late in the day and the sun, which had been blazing white during the long, hot, afternoon, was turning from pale yellow to bright orange as it dipped toward the western horizon.

"Hey, Deputy," Lattimore shouted. "How 'bout we make camp for the night? My ass is that sore from ridin' that I'm near 'bout to split in two."

"We'll be goin' on through 'til we reach Barlow," Lance replied.

"What? Are you serious? Look here, you can't treat me this way. I got rights."

"So did John Tuttle have rights," Lance said.

"John Tuttle? Who the hell is John Tuttle?"

"You don't know? That was the man you killed in Sweetwater."

"I didn't take the time to learn the sonofabitch's name," Lattimore said. "Why should I? After all, there wasn't nothin' personal in it. I mean, I wasn't mad at him or anything. It's just that things like that happen ever' now an' again, and it was that fella's time to go."

"You say that almost as if you consider yourself an instrument of destiny."

Lattimore snorted what may have been a laugh. "An instrument of destiny," he said. "Yeah, I kind'a like that."

"You're a blasphemous bastard, I'll give you that."

"How much farther is it to Barlow, anyway?" "If we keep goin', we'll make it sometime before dawn."

"Before dawn? What the hell? Do you mean to tell me you're plannin' on ridin' all night long?"

"Yep."

"I don't want to tell you how to do your job, Deputy, but what if I was to suddenly decide to make a break for it in the middle of the night? You really think you are a good enough shot to bring me down in the dark?"

"It doesn't make any difference whether I am or not."

"Don't the possibility that I might get away bother you?"

"Nope."

"Why not?"

"You talk too much," Lance said laconically. The two men rode on for another forty-five minutes while the sun dropped lower, and lower still, purpling the clouds and filling the notches of the canyons with evening haze. There was no sound other than the clatter of shod hooves upon the rocky ground. Then, finally, just before the light began to fade, Lance called out to his prisoner. "Hold it up," he said.

"Ah, that's more like it," Lattimore replied. "We're goin' to stop, ain't we?"

Lance rode closer to Lattimore, then looped a rope around his prisoner's neck. He drew the rope tight and, with a start, Lattimore realized that the noose was tied with a hangman's knot.

"Hey! Hey, what the hell is this?" he asked. He raised his hands to feel the rope.

"Leave it alone!" Lance ordered.

"What is this? You've got a hangman's noose around my neck!"

"I guess I do at that. But you may as well get used to it. I'm sure you'll be seeing it again after the judge gets through with you."

"You can't do this! This here is no different from a lynching! What if I was to fall off my horse? What if my horse was to stumble? With this knot behind me, I could break my neck!"

"Don't fall off your horse," Lance said easily. "And don't let your horse stumble."

"You…you sonofabitch! This is why you don't care whether you can shoot well enough to hit me in the dark! You don't have to. As long as I've got this rope around my neck, I won't be goin' anywhere!"

"That's the general idea," Lance agreed.

The two men rode on through the long night. Sometime after midnight, sleep began pulling at Lance. His eyes grew heavy and he began nodding off. On two occasions his head fell forward and the jerk woke him up so that there was no harm done. The third time, however, he jerked awake just in time to see Lattimore slipping his neck out of the noose.

"Hey!" Lance shouted, and startled, Lattimore

pushed the rope up and over his head. He slapped his legs against the side of his horse, intending to bolt away, but the horse was as tired as the riders, and his response wasn't fast enough to give Lattimore the edge he needed. Lance rode after him and caught up with him within less than fifty yards. Lance, who was a powerfully built man, leaned over toward his prisoner and hit him with a club-like fist. Lattimore was knocked from his saddle.

Lance jumped down and jerked Lattimore back to his feet.

"Are you hurt any?" Lance asked. "Any broken bones?"

"No," Lattimore answered sullenly.

"Too bad," Lance replied. "I must be losing my touch." He pointed to Lattimore's horse. "Get back up there. And if you try to get away again, I'll tie you in your saddle, belly down. You want to ride like that, all night?"

"No," Lattimore said again.

Lance swung into his own saddle, then looped the hangman's noose around Lattimore's neck again and held the rope while Lattimore remounted. "All right," he said. "Let's go."

The sun wasn't yet up when the two tired riders rode into Barlow, but there were some houses where the occupants were already up for the start of their long, busy day. Lanterns burned in the kitchens of these houses as the women prepared breakfast. The enticing aroma of bacon and coffee, eggs and biscuits, wafted out into the dark, empty street, reminding Lance that he was hungry.

"Lattimore, you want me to send some breakfast over to you?" he asked.

"No," Lattimore grumbled. "All I want to do is get some sleep."

"Have it your own way." They reached the marshal's office and Lance climbed down, still holding the end of the rope. "All right, you can get down now," he said.

The two men walked into the marshal's office, then to the jail in back. Both cells were occupied by men Lance knew well. They were local citizens who, while the best of friends sober, often got into fights when they were drunk. They were kept in separate cells to keep them from fighting, but Lance was sure they were either sober enough, or hung over enough, to make any more fighting unlikely, so he moved them both into one cell, leaving the other cell free for Lattimore.

"In there," he said, holding the door open for his prisoner, then clanging the door shut and locking it, after Lattimore stepped inside. "You sure you don't want me to send any breakfast over to you?"

"I'll eat when the other prisoners eat," Lattimore said. "Just get the hell out of here and let me get some sleep."

"Glad to oblige," Lance replied, hanging the key ring back on the wall hook. "I've had about as much of your company as I want."

After taking care of his prisoner, Lance unsaddled the two horses, gave them both a brushing, food and water. By the time he was finished with all that, the sky in the east was beginning to glow pink.

George Toomey was asleep on the back stoop of the Easy Pickin's Saloon. Toomey was the town drunk and though, under the ordinances of the town, he could have been arrested for public drunkenness almost anytime Dan Efrem or Lance Chaney wanted to press the issue, it was seldom done. That was because Toomey was a benign drunk who never bothered anyone. In the summertime Toomey preferred sleeping outside and as long as he stayed out of the way he was allowed to do so. In the winter, when it was cold, Toomey slept in a jail cell, but the cell door was never locked and he let himself in or out at will.

Toomey sat up as Lance stepped up onto the back stoop. He rubbed his eyes and saw that the sun was just beginning to come up.

"Just getting in, Deputy?"

"Yes," Lance said.

"Oh, it is a cruel world that will make a man work all night," Toomey observed. Then he chuckled. "But then, it is a cruel world that will make a man work at all."

"Isn't that the truth?" Lance chuckled. "By the way, I'm about to fix myself a little breakfast. Would you care for a bite?"

Toomey shook his head. "Thank you, no," he said.

"Is it my cooking, or what?" Lance asked. "My prisoner didn't want anything to eat, either."

"I have nothing against your cooking, Deputy," Toomey replied. "It's just much too early for food, that's all." He chuckled. "Besides, I never like to eat on an empty stomach."

Lance laughed appreciatively, then went on into the kitchen where he fried himself a couple of slices of bacon, and scrambled three eggs. After that he went up to the second floor where he kept a room, then to bed for a much-needed rest.

CHAPTER 3

THE OUTLAW, RUFUS BLANTON, WAS A product of his times. One hundred years earlier, when men of strength had the advantage in any altercation, Rufus Blanton would have had no choice but to acquiesce, meekly. Today, however, strong men quailed before the weak, if the weak also happened to be accomplished gunmen. Rufus Blanton was a small man who was not only an accomplished gunman, but also had a cold-blooded disregard for the sanctity of life. Such a trait had made him particularly dangerous.

Despite the fact that Rufus Blanton was one of the most feared men around, there was nothing about his appearance which would arrest someone's attention. He was short and slender, with squinting eyes that were cold and gray. On first seeing him, a few women tended to find him attractive. After closer scrutiny, however, they would shy away from him. They couldn't always identify what turned them away. It was as if there were some slight imperfection in his makeup, like flawed crystal, not immediately discernible, but there, nevertheless.

Rufus Blanton's rather unprepossessing appearance enabled him to blend in easily with the public anytime he wanted. There had been many times over the last few years when he had sat quietly in a restaurant, or in the corner of a saloon, listening to people talk about him, unaware that he was just a few feet from them.

He had done that last night. He had sat in a public restaurant in Risco, eating his supper, while other patrons of the cafe carried on innocent conversations, blissfully unaware that they were in company with one of the most skilled and brutal gunmen of all time. During such times Rufus normally paid as little attention to the people around him as they paid to him. Last night, however, the situation was different. Last night, as he lingered over his dinner of baked ham and boiled potatoes, he couldn't help but overhear the attempts of a small, rather mousy-looking man to make himself look important in the eyes of the attractive young waitress.

"I'm afraid I won't be able to take my lunch here tomorrow, Miss Kirby," the man was saying.

"Oh, Mr. Adams? Well, if you've found a better place," the waitress replied.

"No, no, it isn't that. It isn't that at all," Adams said. "It's just that, well, I'll be busy tomorrow. I'll be handling something for the bank, where I am employed."

"Well, I'm sure it must be important," Miss Kirby said.

"Oh, indeed it is, Miss Kirby, indeed it is," Adams said. "Actually, it is a secret. But I suppose I can tell you. Tomorrow, I will be on board the stage for Barlow. My employer is entrusting me with three thousand dollars in negotiable paper money to be delivered to the bank over there. I will keep the money on my person and I will be totally responsible for its safe delivery."

"Won't you be frightened to be carrying that much money?" Miss Kirby asked.

"Frightened? Not at all, Miss Kirby, not at all," Adams said. "You see, though I do not normally do so, I will be carrying a firearm tomorrow. And should I see anyone casting a covetous glance toward the money valise, why I shall simply make certain that he sees the firearm and is thus rendered cognizant of the risks that would be undertaken in any attempt to steal the money."

"Oh, Mr. Adams, please be careful," Miss Kirby

said. "I would simply die if something happened to you."

"Would you, Miss Kirby?" Adams asked, unable to differentiate between what was a polite response, said for effect, and Miss Kirby's true feelings.

"But of course," Miss Kirby replied, not realizing that the bank clerk was taking her mildly flirtatious remarks seriously.

Ruthless paid for his meal then left the restaurant as quietly as he could. After the debacle with the aborted train robbery, it would seem that his luck was about to change. When the stage made its run to Barlow the next morning, he would be waiting for it. If the mousy-looking man was telling the truth, there would be three thousand dollars, just for the taking.

That was last night. This morning Ruthless had already begun to put his plan into operation, and he was standing at the top of Crowley's Pass, waiting for the Risco stage to come lumbering through. Though he had been somewhat nondescript in his mode of dress last night, Ruthless was now wearing what he considered to be his "working clothes." He was wearing a black hat with a silver headband, from which protruded a small red feather. In addition, he wore a black leather vest, worked with rawhide and silver conches, and a red, flannel shirt. Hanging low in a quick-draw holster on the right side of a bullet-studded belt was an ivory-handled Colt .44. It wasn't merely a vain affectation which caused him to dress so. It was a means of setting apart the "public" Rufus Blanton and the "private" Rufus Blanton. Ruthless the outlaw was known and often described by the colorful garb he wore. Such association made it much easier for him to slip in and out of town in more nondescript clothing.

From the rock overhang where he was standing, Ruthless looked down into the valley, some thirty-five hundred feet below. There, just coming up out of the early-morning mist, was the stage from Risco. Ruthless had actually chosen to wait for it at the turnout just below the crest of the pass because it would be a long, exhausting climb for the team. That meant that the driver would have to halt the horses here to give them a rest.

From the position and progress of the coach, Ruthless knew that it would take at least half an hour for it to reach his vantage point, so he took some jerky from his saddlebag, unhooked the canteen, then sat under a tree to have his breakfast and read the newspaper he had picked up last night:

TRAIN ROBBERY THWARTED BY PASSENGER

A train robbery, believed to have been attempted by Rufus Blanton and two of his confederates, was thwarted on the week ultimate, by the quick and courageous action of one of the passengers. The resultant gunplay left two of the would-be robbers dead and the third, thought to be Rufus Blanton, fleeing for his life.

According to witnesses, Rufus Blanton's two confederates entered the train cars with the intention of divesting each and every passenger of his possessions. However, one of the passengers, later identified as Buck Chaney, refused to be bullied by the strong-arm tactics of the brigands and he pulled his pistol and awaited the opportunity to do battle.

That opportunity came sooner than the villains expected when there was an exchange of gunfire between Mr. Chaney and the two robbers who had boarded the train. When the smoke was cleared the two robbers lay dead in the aisle of the train car, and Mr. Chaney, having gotten the better of the dispute, was running through the darkness to issue a challenge to the remaining robber.

According to a statement rendered by the train conductor, the night outside the cars was lit up by the muzzle-flashes of the two men firing at each other. The two men were locked in desperate battle and although Mr. Chaney didn't have as much success with Rufus Blanton as he had with the two desperadoes whom he had earlier killed, he did best the outlaw in the ensuing competition, for Ruthless, according to the conductor, "turned tail and ran."

"So," Ruthless said, chuckling as he read the article. "I have turned tail and run, have I? Well, Mr. Buck Chaney, we'll see who the ultimate victor in our little competition is."

By the time Ruthless finished looking at the newspaper, he was startled by the pop of the driver's whip. He realized then that the stage was nearly upon him, so he got up, put the newspaper away, mounted his horse and rode back into the trees, just out of sight.

"Whoa, hold up there, horses," the driver shouted, pulling on the reins. The stage rumbled to a stop and the driver set the brake. "Fellas," the driver called down to his passengers. "We gotta let these here animals get a good blow before we start down the other side. And since we ain't got no ladies on board, I reckon this here would be as good a place as any for you'ns to take a leak iffen you're of a mind to."

Three men climbed down from the stage. One was a rancher, well-built, with broad shoulders and big hands. The second was a gambler, nattily dressed in accordance with his trade. The third man was the same clerk Ruthless had seen last night. He was small and mousy-looking, and wearing little wire-rim glasses. He was carrying a valise which he kept clutched tightly to his chest. Whether or not he was actually carrying a pistol as he had told the waitress last night, Ruthless couldn't tell…at least not from his current vantage point.

"Seth, you wanna give me a hand here?" the driver asked, encountering some difficulty in adjusting a harness.

"That damn thing come loose again?" the shotgun guard replied, leaning his gun against the front wheel. "You ought to do somethin' about that."

"I'm goin' to," the driver replied. "When we get to Barlow, I'm gonna replace it."

When Ruthless saw the gun put aside and the guard busy with the driver, he smiled. This was just the opportunity he had been looking for.

"Howdy, folks," he said, speaking in a gravelly voice, as he rode out toward the coach. He had taken the precaution of masking the bottom half of his face with his bandanna, but that didn't fool the shotgun guard.

"It's Rufus Blanton!" Seth shouted, and he started toward his gun.

Ruthless waited until the guard had already picked up his shotgun and swung it toward him before he shot. The heavy .44-caliber slug from his pistol raised dust on Seth's shirt as it went in, then sprayed blood out his back and onto the side of the coach, as it exited.

"You sonofabitch!" the driver shouted, running for the shotgun. He grabbed it from the guard's hands, then swung it around toward Ruthless, pulling the trigger as he did so.

The driver shot too quickly and the pellets flew harmlessly into the trees. With an evil laugh, Ruthless pulled the trigger again. His shot hit the driver under his right eye and the driver went down, dead before he hit the ground.

The entire encounter had taken no more than a few seconds, and during that time the three passengers had stood in place, frozen by their fear. When Ruthless turned his gun toward them, they all raised their hands.

"No, don't shoot!" the gambler yelled.

"Anyone else want to make a try for the shotgun?" Ruthless growled.

"No! No, we're not going to do anything," the gambler assured him.

"Good, good. That means you have a mite more sense than these two galoots had. You, Mr. Adams," he said, pointing to the clerk. "Toss that satchel over to me."

"How...how do you know my name?" Adams asked in total shock.

"You'd be surprised at what I know. Now, hand me the satchel like I said."

"What...what do you want this for?" Adams

squeaked, wrapping both arms around it and pulling it closer to his chest. "There isn't anything in here but a change of clothes."

Very pointedly, Ruthless pulled the kerchief down so Adams could see his smile.

"Well, now, that ain't exactly what you was tellin' that sweet little waitress in the cafe last night, is it? I do believe I heard you tellin' her that you would be carryin' over three thousand dollars."

"You...you were there?" Adams asked, incredulously.

"At the table right beside you. And I heard every word."

"No, you couldn't have been. I would have seen you."

"Not if I didn't want to be seen," Ruthless said. "Now," he added pointedly. "Hand me the valise."

"There's nothing in the valise, really."

"All right, open it up. If you're tellin' the truth, I won't do nothin' to you. But if you're lyin' to me, mister, I'm goin' to kill you where you stand."

"No! No! Don't shoot me. All right, all right, there is some money in the bag."

"How much?"

"Th...three thousand, two hundred and twenty-five dollars," the clerk stammered.

Ruthless smiled again, and this time his smile was more genuine. "Do you see how easy that was?" he asked. He held his left hand out. "Bring the bag over here to me," he ordered.

While his two fellow passengers stood by with their hands up, Adams walked over and handed the valise to Ruthless. Ruthless took it with his left hand and hooked it onto his saddle pommel.

"Thank you," he said. "Now, get back over there with the others and put your hands up." The clerk did as he was instructed.

"Stay that way for five minutes...all of you," Ruthless ordered. "My partner is over there in the trees, with a rifle pointed at you. If any of you move before the five minutes is up, he'll blow your head off."

"What...what do we do after the five minutes is up?" Adams asked.

Ruthless chuckled. "Do? Why, Mr. Adams, I personally, don't give a damn what you do. But if I was in your shoes, I'd see if I couldn't drive the stage on into town."

Ruthless slapped his legs against the side of his horse, then rode off into the tree line. The moment he was out of sight, the rancher lowered his hands. "Let's see if they're both dead," he suggested.

"Are you crazy? There's a man in the trees with a rifle pointed at us!" Adams squealed in fear.

"Then let the sonofabitch shoot," the rancher growled. "I'm not going to let these fellas just lie here." He squatted down to look at them. "The driver's dead," he said. "But the guard's still alive. Help me get him inside, we've got to get him to a doctor."

The gambler lowered his hands and started to help the rancher lift the injured guard. Only Mr. Adams continued to hold his hands up, all the while keeping his eyes tightly closed in fear.

"You're going to get us all killed!" he whimpered. "Please, do what he told us to do."

"You think you can drive this thing?" the gambler asked, ignoring the clerk's plea. He and the rancher put the wounded guard inside the coach.

"I don't know. I've never done it before, but I have handled four-hitch wagons," the rancher replied. "Two more can't be that hard."

"What about him?" the gambler pointed to the dead driver.

"We'll put him on top."

Straining against the weight, the two men lifted the dead driver all the way to the top of the stage. Then the rancher and the gambler climbed onto the driver's seat and the rancher picked up the reins. He looked around at Mr. Adams who was still standing alongside with his hands in the air.

"You comin' or stayin'?" he asked.

Adams opened his eyes then and saw that both the driver and the guard had been picked up. He looked back toward the tree line, studying it intently.

The rancher released the brake.

"No! No, wait! I'll go!" the clerk shouted, scrambling quickly to get into the coach. The wounded guard groaned as the coach lurched forward. The clerk held on for dear life.

CHAPTER 4

IT HAD BEEN NEARLY SIX O'CLOCK BY THE time Lance Chaney finally got to bed. Now it was nearly ten, but as he lay in his bed listening to the morning sounds of Barlow drift in through his window, he knew that he had already slept as much as he was going to.

Just across the street, in the empty lot between Poindexter's Emporium and Bixby's Leathergoods where the new hardware store was going, someone was chopping down a tree with the heavy thump, thump, thump of an axe. Up the street the smithy was shaping an iron wheel rim at his forge and his hammer made a ringing sound on the off-beat of the thumping axe. Downstairs, Sam Goodbody was sweeping the front porch of the Easy Pickin's Saloon, adding the scratch of his broom to the beat of the axe and ring of the hammer. Though unintended, the result was a rhythmic composition; thump, ring, scratch-scratch-scratch...thump, ring, scratch-scratch-scratch.

There were other sounds as well; a freight wagon moving slowly down the street, some children playing a game of hide-and-seek, and a sign, squeaking in the morning breeze. Finally, all of the sounds combined to drive Lance out of his bed, so, with a groan of resignation, he walked over to the chest of drawers and poured water from the big, porcelain pitcher into the basin. He looked at himself in the mirror, trying to make up his mind if he should shave or grow a beard. With a shrug of his powerful shoulders, he decided to take the dark, overnight growth off, so he picked up his mug and began working up a lather.

He had just finished shaving when he heard loud shouts coming up from the street.

"Hold up! There was a hold up! Turn out, ever'body, turn out! The stage was robbed!" someone shouted.

Lance moved over to the window and pulled the curtain aside so he could look down onto the street. The stage rumbled by just underneath and he recognized Andy McGinnis, lying out on top. The man handling the reins was Charley Bates, a rancher whose spread was nearby, and the man riding shotgun beside him was Johnny Karpo, a local gambler. Lance didn't see Seth, the regular shotgun guard.

Lance heard someone pounding loudly on his door. Wiping the rest of the shaving lather off his face, he walked over to jerk it open. Sam Goodbody, the Easy Pickin's bartender, was standing in the hallway.

"Oh, you're up already," Sam said. "I just thought I'd come tell you the stage was robbed. That's in case you'd want to get down to the marshal's office."

"Yeah, thanks," Lance said.

"'Course, bein' as you brought in a prisoner last night, I don't reckon you'd really have to go.

"I reckon not," Lance said. He strapped on his gun belt, then reached for his hat.

"But I figured you'd be wantin' to," Sam added.

"I reckon so," Lance said. He closed the door to his room behind him, then followed Sam down the hall toward the stairs.

"Lance?"

Lance turned toward the sound of the woman's voice and saw Lily Montgomery standing in her door at the far end of the hall. Lily owned the saloon.

"Morning, Lily," Lance said, touching the brim of his hat.

"What is it? What's all the commotion?"

"The stage was held up, Miss Lily," Sam said, answering before Lance could. "There was a shootin' too. When the coach come in, the driver was layin' out on top an' the shotgun guard, why, he was inside."

"Oh, the poor men," Lily said. "Lance, be careful."

Lance smiled. "You know me, Lily," he said. "Careful is my middle name."

Lance left the saloon then hurried across the street toward the gathering crowd. Nearly everyone in town had been drawn to the stage by the curious nature of its arrival. By now the driver and the guard had been taken from the coach and were stretched out on the boardwalk in front of the marshal's office. Doc Presnell was kneeling down beside the guard, feeling for a pulse in his neck. He wasn't wasting his time with the driver. With his eyes open and opaque, and a big, black hole in his cheek, it didn't require a doctor to see that Andy McGinnis was very obviously dead.

"Mornin', Lance," Marshal Dan Efrem said. "I see you found Lattimore. Good job."

"It was easy enough, seeing as he was right where you said he would be," Lance answered. "What do you know about this?" he asked, indicating the two men Doctor Presnell was working on.

"Not much, I'm afraid," Dan said. "Like you, I just got here." The marshal was standing just outside his office with his arms folded across his chest, watching the doctor at work.

"Can I use your door, Dan?" Doc Presnell asked, looking up at the marshal. "We've got to get Seth over to my place and we're goin' to need something to carry him on."

"Yes, of course," Dan replied, and he nodded toward two other men who, quickly, began to take the door to the marshal's office off its hinges, so it could be used as a carrying board. "Is Seth going to make it, Doc?"

"I don't know," Doc Presnell said. "He's got a chance. The bullet went through him high enough that it missed all his vitals, but you never can tell with gunshot wounds."

"Let me know how he's doin', will you, Doc?" Dan asked.

"Sure thing, Marshal."

Dan looked back at Lance. "What time did you get in with Lattimore?"

"About five-thirty or six."

"Pretty short night for you, wasn't it?"

"I suppose so, but I'll be all right after a cup of coffee."

"There's a pot on the stove," Dan offered.

"I'll get some directly," Lance replied. "Soon as we get a handle on things."

Dan looked over at the gambler. "Johnny, you want to tell us what happened?"

"It was Rufus Blanton," Johnny said. "Ruthless?

Are you sure?" Dan asked.

"Yeah, I'm sure. I've seen him a couple of times before."

"What about you two?" Dan asked. "You go along with that?"

"I've never seen him for real," the rancher replied. "But I've seen dodgers on him and I'd say that's who it was. Besides, I heard Seth call out his name, just before he was shot."

"It was him, all right," the clerk said.

"You've seen him before, have you?" Dan asked.

"Well, uh, no," the clerk admitted. "But I have heard him described. And this was him, all right. I don't have the slightest doubt about it."

The undertaker's wagon arrived. The driver halted the team and set the brake, then looked over at Dan.

"If you're through with the body, Marshal, I'll take it now," the driver said. He was wearing a long, black coat and a pair of striped pants.

"Sure thing, Mr. Albritton, but maybe you'd better hold off on doin' anything more with it 'til we hear from the widow," Dan suggested. "I reckon Mrs. McGinnis will be wantin' him brought back home."

"I've no doubt that she will. I'll just get in touch with my colleague over in Risco and keep him on ice until I get further instructions," Albritton explained.

Dan turned his attention back to the three passengers. "I'll tell you folks what has me puzzled. What I don't understand is, why someone like Rufus Blanton would want to hold up the stage between Risco and Barlow in the first place. Why, there couldn't have been more'n ten or fifteen dollars between everybody on board, could there? I mean this stage doesn't even carry a strongbox."

"The money wasn't in a strongbox, it was in a valise," Karpo said.

"The money? What money?"

"A little over three thousand dollars. This fella here, was carrying it."

"What were you doing with so much money?" Lance asked.

The bank clerk pulled himself up importantly. "My name is C. D. Adams, Marshal," he explained. "I work for the Bank of Risco and I was overseeing a species transfer to the Bank of Barlow."

"Damn," Lance said. "Someone slipped up somewhere. Those transfers are supposed to be kept secret. I wonder how Ruthless found out."

"I... I really don't know," Adams stammered.

"The hell you don't," Karpo replied. "You were spoutin' it off all over the restaurant at supper last night. Everybody heard you. They were talking about it down at the saloon."

"Yeah," Bates said. "I even heard about it down at the feeder lot."

"Is that true?"

"I…I suppose so," Adams replied.

"What the hell? Why didn't you just take out an ad in the newspapers?" Lance asked.

"I…I didn't think it would do any harm," Adams insisted. "I was just trying to make an impression on Miss Kirby."

"Miss Kirby?"

"She's the waitress at the City Pig Cafe," Adams explained.

"So, because you were trying to make an impression on a waitress, you babbled all over the place that you would be carrying a lot of money between banks," Dan said scornfully. "And as a result, one man was killed and another may die. In addition to that, you lost all your employer's money."

"I didn't know anything like this would happen," Adams whined. "Honest I didn't."

"Yeah, well, I'm not the one you have to answer to," Dan said. "If I were you I'd get myself down to the bank and start making explanations there."

"You need me anymore, Dan?" Karpo asked.

"No, I guess not. You can go too, Bates," Dan replied. "And thanks for bringing in the stage…you did a good job."

"By the way, Lance, when is your brother going to get back?" Karpo asked. "We've got a few more hands of poker to play."

"Your guess as to when Buck will get back is as good as mine," Lance answered with a little laugh. "You know how he is. There's always another town to see, another hole-card to draw to, and another bar girl to spark."

Karpo chuckled. "That's Buck, all right. It's sure hard to pin him down. I swear, I never in my life saw any two brothers as different as you two. To begin with, you don't even look alike; you're three inches taller and fifty pounds heavier. You're dark, he's light, you're settled, he's wild, the only thing alike is that a man with good sense wouldn't want to get on the bad side of either one of you. Anyway, next time you see Buck, tell him he owes me a couple of games so I can get even."

"I'll tell him," Lance promised.

"Come on in, Lance," Dan invited. "You can drink your coffee while I'm gettin' ready."

"Getting ready? Getting ready for what?"

"I'm goin' after him."

"There's no call to do that, Dan," Lance said. "The fact is, you don't really even have the authority to go after him. The town council hired you to keep the peace here in Barlow, not go running through the countryside chasing road agents."

"I know why I was hired, Lance. But I got a special want for this fella," Dan replied. He looked over at Lance. "You, of all people, should understand that."

"Yeah," Lance replied as he took a swallow of coffee and studied Dan over the rim of his cup. "Yeah, I guess I do."

The "understanding" Dan mentioned, referred to the fact that Lance Chaney and his brother Buck had arrived in Barlow, Texas a little over a year earlier, hard on the trail of the men who had raped and killed their sister. They had started on their quest from opposite sides, for Lance had been a captain in the Union Army, while Buck was a lieutenant in the Confederacy. However, their past differences were put aside long enough for them to settle the score with their sister's killers, though it ultimately took a range war to get that accomplished.

The range war was over now, but there were still enough gunfighters, holdup men, gamblers, prospectors, cowboys and wild women to keep the place jumping, and to keep the Chaney boys interested. To the two brothers, Barlow meant two different things. Buck, being younger, quicker-tempered, and faster with a gun, rather enjoyed the excitement of the town. He hung around to take maximum advantage of all the experiences a place like Barlow had to offer, supporting himself by his wits...gambling mostly, though he had done a little bartending and had even hired himself out as a shotgun guard on a few occasions. Buck was friendly with all the women, but so far he had managed to avoid getting too close to any woman in particular.

Lance was the more settled of the two and he stayed around Barlow because, as he said, "Everyone has to be somewhere." There were those, however, who suggested that Lance stayed in Barlow because of Lily Montgomery, the owner of the Easy Pickin's saloon. Actually, there was a great deal of truth to that suggestion. Lily was a beautiful woman and not at all like the average sporting house madam.

Lily could remember the days when she was the daughter of a wealthy Mississippi planter and the "Belle of the County." She still had the airs of a fine lady and cowboys who were visiting the saloon for the first time and who knew nothing of Lily's background, seemed to sense that, and react to it.

Lance and Lily had an understanding of sorts, though the parameters of that understanding had not been fully explored. Lance certainly wasn't ready to discuss marriage and he didn't consider himself engaged. Also, since their relationship had never actually been articulated they were free, technically, to see others. It was obvious to everyone, however, that while Lily ran a bar and sporting house and served drinks and a smile to men, she was interested only in Lance Chaney. It was just as obvious that Lance, who had a polite smile for all the working girls of the Easy Pickin's Saloon, was really interested in sharing his table and drinks only with Lily.

When the job was offered to him, Lance pinned on the star of deputy marshal. The new marshal, Dan Efrem, needed a deputy, and Lance Chaney needed work. What made the situation somewhat unusual was that Lance was one of those responsible for getting Efrem to come to Barlow in the first place.

Dan Efrem was a well-known and highly-respected law officer, a former Texas Ranger and United States Marshal. He was hired by the town of Barlow in the hopes of cleaning up Barlow's image, tarnished by the range war and several months of control by crooked elements. Efrem had been successful in his efforts, as evidenced by the fact that the criminal elements now knew that Barlow was a town to avoid. He had won the respect of the entire town, and the friendship of his deputy.

Lance watched as Dan took a Winchester down from the rack and started sliding .44-.40 cartridges into the loading tube. Marshal Efrem was thin and wiry, with gray hair, light blue eyes, and a full, handlebar moustache. His face was weathered and his eyes were old, but Lance knew that anyone who underestimated him would be making a big mistake. He was lightning-fast with a gun...so fast that even Buck had once confided to Lance that he would never want to go up against him.

"Who do you think we ought to get to watch the place while we're gone?" Lance asked.

"Watch the place? What are you talking about? You're going to watch it," Dan said. He was checking the loads in his pistol, turning the cylinder one click at a time and looking into each chamber.

"I can't watch it. I'm going with you…after Rufus Blanton."

"Don't need you."

"I want to help."

Dan looked at Lance and smiled. "No offense, Lance, but you'd just get in the way," he said.

"Besides, we're old friends, Ruthless and me." With both his rifle and pistol loaded, Dan put a couple of extra boxes of shells into one of the saddlebags.

"Friends?"

"Well, I wouldn't say we are exactly friends," Dan said with a smile that didn't quite reach his eyes. "But we are acquainted. You see, the only time he has ever been in jail, I put him there. That is, my partner and I. But six months ago, Rufus Blanton was paroled out of jail. About a month after that, Johnny Miller was killed."

"Your partner?"

"Yeah," Dan said. "He was the one with me when we arrested Ruthless the last time. Of course it's never been proved that Ruthless killed Johnny, but there's no doubt in my mind."

"If he did kill him, have you stopped to think that there might be more to this than just a stage robbery? Ruthless might be trying to set you up."

"That's true," Dan admitted, standing up and tossing the saddlebags over his shoulder. He clutched the Winchester in his left hand, while with his right, he reached out to shake hands. "Well, I'm off," he said. "You'll keep an eye on things for me around here?"

"You can count on it," Lance said.

Dan smiled. "Oh, I do, all the time," he replied. As he started out the door he pointed back toward the jail cells with the jerk of his thumb. "By the way, you can let Cooper and Ellis out," he said. "I should'a let 'em go half an hour ago, but I got busy."

"I'll take care of it," Lance said.

When Lance went into the back of the jail a few minutes later, he saw Cooper looking through the back window while Ellis was sitting on the bunk, holding his head in his hands. In the other cell, Lattimore was sound asleep, his uneaten breakfast still sitting on the table. Flies were buzzing around the cold eggs and rubbery-looking bacon.

"What was all the ruckus a while ago?" Cooper asked when Lance started opening the cell door. "I couldn't make nothin' out from back here."

"The Risco stage was held up," Lance said. "They

killed the driver and shot up the guard." "Who did it?"

"Rufus Blanton."

"The marshal go after him?"

"Yep."

Cooper picked up his hat and stepped through the door to freedom. He shivered a little. "Better him than me. Ruthless is one evil sonofabitch."

"You know Rufus Blanton?" Lance asked.

"I've seen 'im," Cooper replied. "We've both seen 'im, ain't we, Ellis?"

"Yeah," Ellis agreed. "We seen 'im in a little ruckus up at San Angelo. Went up against two men, he did, and killed 'em both 'fore either one of 'em could get off so much as one shot. He's fast, Deputy. He can clear leather faster'n anyone I ever seen."

"Yes, well, I reckon Dan can handle himself. By the way, how about you two not raising a ruckus tonight? As you can see, I brought in a real prisoner, and I'm goin' to have my hands full until Dan gets back. I'm not going to have time to be mollycoddling drunks."

Cooper chuckled. "You don't have to worry about me an' Ellis gettin' drunk and fightin' tonight," he said. "Both of us done spent all our poke."

"Good," Lance said.

A little while later, Lance checked in at Doc Presnell's office and found that Seth was holding his own. He also checked at the telegraph office where he learned that the driver's widow did want his body sent back to Risco, so he went down to Albritton's Funeral Parlor to pass the word. Then, at around noon, he dropped in at the Easy Pickin's where he knew his lunch would already be laid out on the table in the rear.

"Hello," Lily said, greeting him with a smile.

"Hello, yourself."

"Mind if I join you?"

"Please do."

It was ritualistic. The table was already set for two, as it was nearly every day. Lance held the chair for Lily, then he sat down across from her and forked a pork chop onto his plate.

"Heard from Buck, lately?" Lily asked.

"Only what I read in the papers," Lance replied. "And that was a couple of weeks ago. Seems he was quite a hero to the folks on that train."

"And why not?" Lily replied. "Your brother is a man of heroic qualities."

Lance laughed. "What are you trying to do, Lily? Make me jealous of Buck?"

"If I thought it would work," Lily replied, her comment sounding more serious than she wanted it to. She cleared her throat and pushed on, lest her talk make Lance uncomfortable. "Anyway, the reason I asked is, I talked to someone today who ran into Buck, a few days ago," Lily said.

"Since the train incident?"

"Yes."

"Where is he?"

"He was in Bitter Springs playing poker, when the fellow I talked to, saw him."

"He's been gone quite a spell this time. The cards must be running well for him," Lance said.

CHAPTER 5

BITTER SPRINGS ONLY HAD ONE STREET.
It started as a scratch in the desert, ran west between two rows of well-constructed wooden
buildings: general stores, leathergoods stores, a
couple of laundries, and a disproportionate number
of saloons and gambling halls, then it turned into
another scratch in the desert on the far side.

One of the more popular saloons was the Gilded
Cage, located right in the middle of town. The Gilded Cage got its name from the painting behind the
bar, a three-by-six-foot oil canvas showing a nude
woman sitting on a perch in a gilded cage.

Buck Chaney, who was playing cards in the
Gilded Cage, laughed at something one of the bar
girls said to him, and his bright blue eyes literally
sparkled in merriment. He brushed a fall of blond
hair away from his forehead, then winked at one of
the girls.

"One card in the hole, a pair of deuces and a Jack showing," he said. "I need another deuce or another Jack. Now, which one of you is going to give me a kiss for luck?"

"I'll give you a kiss," one of the girls offered.

"I will too."

"I said it first."

Buck laughed. "My lips won't get tired," he said. "I can take one from each of you."

It was no mystery why the girls were hanging around the lean, but wiry-tough young man. Not only was he very good looking and full of fun and laughter, he was also spending freely. Since arriving in town day before yesterday, he had been having a phenomenal run of luck with the cards.

Dutifully, both girls kissed him, then he smiled and looked around the table at the other card players.

"Gents, I'll be payin' twenty dollars for the next card," Buck said, pushing his money out to the center of the table.

A huge bull of a man with no neck, a drooping black mustache and cold, fishlike eyes sat directly across the table from Buck.

"It ain't your bet, Mister," he said, pointing to his cards. "Can't you see I got me a pair of eights showin'? And I'm bettin' five dollars."

"No problem, I'll just raise it to twenty," Buck said easily.

"What are you tryin' to do? Buy the pot?" the big man growled.

"This here hand has already got too rich for me," one of the other players said. He folded his cards on the table in front of him and the others around the table came to the same decision.

"Peters you foldin' or playin'?" the dealer asked the fish-eyed man.

"Are you kiddin'? I've got him beat showin'. I'm callin'," Peters replied.

The dealer was one of those who had already dropped out of the hand, and he started to deal.

Buck drew another deuce, giving him three showing. "Well, now, that is pretty," he said.

Peters drew another eight, giving him three showing, and he laughed out loud. "That's prettier," he said. "One hundred dollars, prettier."

As Peters clasped his hands on the table in front of him, Buck saw him, cleverly, change his hole-card with one that he was keeping up his sleeve. Quickly, Buck looked around the table and saw that the fourth eight was already showing in one of the folded hands. Buck smiled. That being the case, it didn't matter whether Peters changed the hole card or not. Buck knew that he had him beaten.

"Well, what about it, ladies' man?" Peters asked derisively. "Are you playin' or has it suddenly got too rich for your blood?"

"I don't see a hundred dollars in front of you," Buck challenged.

"I'm good for it."

"Not to me, you aren't. I've never seen you before today."

"I'm tellin' you, I'm good for it."

"I'm afraid not."

"Wait a minute," Peters said. He looked around the saloon, then saw a couple of his friends and grinned, broadly. "George, Bill, come over here."

The two he called, also mean, rough-looking men, responded to his summons.

"I need you two fellas to stake me enough money to finish this here hand."

The men looked at the cards on the table, then chuckled, and brought out fifty dollars apiece. Given the look of the cards showing, Buck wasn't surprised they agreed to back his opponent, but he was surprised that men so ill-kempt looking would have that much money on them in the first place.

"Now," Peters said, sliding his money into the center of the table. "Like I said, I'm bettin' one hundred dollars."

When Buck hesitated for a second, Peters chuckled, and reached out to rake in the pot.

"It was a pleasure doin' business with you," he said.

"Wait a minute, I'm still playing," Buck replied.

"I was just trying to make up my mind whether I should call, or raise."

"What? Are you crazy?" Peters sputtered. "Can't you see that I got you beat?"

"I guess I'll just call," Buck replied as, with an easy grin, he slid his money into the large pile of bills and coins that was already in the middle of the table.

"I thank you for your donation," Peters laughed, turning over his hole-card. It was another ace, to go with the three eights and one ace he had showing. Buck knew that Peters had pulled the second ace from his shirtsleeve.

"A full house," Peters said. "Aces and eights." Once again, he reached for the pot.

"Sorry," Buck said easily. He turned up his hole card. "But it looks like I win." It was a deuce.

"Four deuces!" someone gasped, and the girls squealed in delight.

"The hell you say!"

Peters' outburst was followed by the crashing sound of a chair tipping over as he stood abruptly. A woman's laughter halted in mid-trill, and the piano player pulled his hands away from the keyboard so that the last three notes of his song hung raggedly, discordantly in the air. All conversation ceased and everyone in the crowded saloon turned toward the cause of the disturbance.

"You sonofabitch! You pulled that deuce from the bottom of the deck!"

"Peters, what are you talking about? How could he have done that?" the dealer asked. "I was the one dealing, not him."

"Yeah?" Peters sputtered. "Well, I don't know how he's doin' it, but this sonofabitch is cheatin'!"

"Interesting that you would accuse me," Buck exclaimed, "when I saw you pull that second ace from your shirtsleeve."

"Don't think you're goin' to get out of it by accusin' me," Peters said. "These fellas know better."

"Do they?" Buck asked. He pointed to the folded hands. "You've got two aces, and I can see two more aces showing." Buck began turning up the down cards of the players who had folded. The second card he turned over was an ace. "Well, now, Mr. Peters, what do you say about that?" he asked.

Peters' frown turned into an evil grin and he wiped the back of his hand across his mustache. "What do I say about it?" he asked. "I say I'm going to beat the hell out of you, you smart mouthed bastard." Peters raised his fists in front of his face and began moving them around in tiny circles. The fists were as huge as sledgehammers.

The table moved and the chairs fell over as the

other players hurried to get out of the way. Buck looked at them.

"I don't suppose any of you want to help me?" Buck suggested to the other players. "After all, he was cheating you, too."

"Maybe he was, Mister," one of the other players said. "But you was the one winnin'."

"Yes," Buck said. He sighed, and dropped his hand to his pistol. "Well, suppose I tell you I don't want to fight you."

Buck heard the metallic click of two pistols being cocked, and he saw that the two men who had loaned Peters money were now backing their investment with drawn pistols.

"You got no choice, woman's man," one of them said. "You either fight back, or you stand there and let Peters drive you down like a nail in a board."

"Well, if I got no choice," Buck said with a shrug of his shoulders. Then, totally unexpectedly, and so quickly that Peters was unable to react to it, Buck sent a whistling punch square into Peters' chin. Peters' neck snapped back and his head rolled back on his shoulders, and he went down, crashing to the floor like a felled oak tree. "Damn!" someone said. "Did you see that?" Peters got up smiling and rubbing his chin.

"Oh, shit," Buck said, quietly. He had put everything he had into that one punch, thinking the element of surprise was his only hope. And yet,

Peters was back on his feet almost as if nothing had happened.

"Well, I see you decided to fight after all," Peters said.

Without bothering to answer him, Buck snapped a good, one-two combination into Peters' face. He scored with a slashing left, then followed it up quickly with a well-thrown right, but Peters just flinched once, and laughed a low, evil laugh.

"Fight! There's a fight goin' on in the saloon!" someone shouted out over the bat wing doors, and within a moment the place was filled with people who had been drawn by the excitement.

"I'm givin' three to one on Peters!" someone shouted, and when he got no takers, he raised the odds. "Five to one! Five to one on Peters!"

"I'll bet two dollars," one of the girls said.

Though Buck was aware of all the byplay going on around him, he was unable to pay much attention to who said what, because he was busy with the task at hand. He was quick enough, of course, to just back away from the fight and leave the saloon. And, because of the disparity in the relative size of the two combatants, most people wouldn't think any less of him for doing so. However, there was more than mere loss of face involved. There was almost three hundred dollars on that table, and if Buck walked away now, he would have to leave the money here. That was all the money he had in the world. There was no way he was going to leave it.

With an angry roar, Peters suddenly charged Buck, and Buck stepped aside, avoiding him like a matador sidestepping a charging bull. And, like a charging bull, Peters slammed into a table, smashing it into kindling. As he was disentangling himself, Buck moved up and sent a whistling blow against Peters' jaw. He scored a direct hit, but if he thought that would bring Peters down, he had another thought coming.

"Stand still, you little sonofabitch!" Peters said, whirling around and swinging wildly at Buck. Buck hadn't expected Peters to counter punch so quickly, and he just barely got out of the way in time. Had Peters connected, it would have been over for Buck with that one punch.

Peters was turned now to face Buck, and they circled around each other for a moment, holding their fists doubled in front of them, each looking for an opening in the other.

Peters swung again, another club-like swing which Buck was able to lean away from. Buck counterpunched, connecting again as he had before. Again, however, Peters was able to laugh it off, and Buck's punches, though thrown with authority, seemed to have no more effect than the bite of a mosquito.

Buck learned quickly that he could hit Peters

anytime he wanted, and though Peters didn't seem to show any immediate reaction to the blows, Buck couldn't help but believe there was some cumulative effect. That suspicion was borne out a few moments later when he saw Peters' eyes begin to puff up, and a lip swell.

Buck started looking for a chance to hit Peters in the nose, timing his left-right, and looking for the right combination. Then he got the opening he was looking for and he sent a whistling right to Peters' nose. Peters let out a yelp of pain as Buck felt the nose go under his hand. The bridge of the nose was crushed and blood started running across Peters' teeth and chin.

Buck knew then that this would be the only chance he would have of ending the fight, so he started looking for another opening, but Peters was protecting it. Peters continued to throw great, heavy swings toward Buck, but Buck was able to avoid them. Then, while looking for another opportunity to hit Peters in the nose, Buck got careless and was caught by the end part of one of Peters' swings. The swing had nearly played itself out so that Buck caught only a portion of the original power of the blow but even that was enough to send him down, flat on his back.

The crowd roared with excitement then, as they waited for Peters to close in for the kill. Peters, with a shout of triumph, rushed toward Buck, then raised one foot with the intention of stomping Buck's head. Buck rolled to one side just as Peters' foot came smashing down where Buck's head had been but a moment before. Then Buck, while still on his back, sent the point of his boot whistling into Peters' crotch.

With a bellow like a pole-axed steer, Peters bent over, grabbing himself as he did so. Buck jumped quickly to his feet, then sent a powerful blow into Peters' Adam's apple. Peters turned blue, then fell through the top of a table. He lay on the floor in the splintered wood, gasping for breath and whimpering in pain.

Breathing hard, Buck walked over to what had been the playing table, still undamaged, and began scooping up his winnings.

"Just what the hell do you think you're doin' there, Mister?" one of the two men who had backed Peters, asked.

Buck looked toward the man and saw that he was still holding his pistol.

"Let him alone," a woman's voice suddenly said. "He won the fight, and the money."

"Missy, you just stay the hell out..." the man started to say, then he let his words stop in midsentence, for the woman who had challenged him was holding a double-barrel, Greener, ten-gauge shot-gun pointed right at him. The woman hauled back on the two hammers of the shotgun. "Hey, hold it!" the man shouted in fear. "Those things have been known to go off!"

"Then drop your gun and let Buck walk out of here," the woman said. "Both of you!" she ordered, looking at the other one as well, though his pistol was still in his holster.

Both pistols clattered to the floor.

"Thanks, Donna," Buck said, as he continued to scoop up the money. He walked over to Donna and the other two bar girls, kissed each one of them while, at the same time, slipping a large bill down the top of her dress. Then, with a smile, he gave a little wave toward the others in the saloon, still stunned by the unexpected result of the fight.

"If you fellas don't mind," he said, "I think I'll be goin' on. This town just isn't fun anymore."

CHAPTER 6

THE RISCO CEMETERY WAS A STARK, TREELESS piece of ground just south of town. There had been several attempts made to plant flowers and though a few of the hardier plants did manage to take root, the overall appearance of the graveyard was little different from the desert that surrounded it. All the grave markers were of wood. Most were in the form of a tablet, though many were shaped like a cross. In a few cases the inscriptions had grown so dim that the most determined effort couldn't identify who lay buried beneath the marker.

There was no such problem with Andy McGinnis' marker, however. It was bright and new, and in addition to the vital information of his name, the date he was born and the date he died, it also had the lines:

A Brave Man
"Cowards die many times.
The brave die but once."

Dan Efrem stayed near the back edge of the Risco graveyard, watching the funeral proceedings. A large mound of dirt was piled up next to the newly opened grave, dark colored against the sun-bleached, rocky ground. Mrs. McGinnis, in her widow's weeds, and with red-rimmed eyes, was quietly sobbing as the preacher intoned the graveside rites.

"For as much as it hath pleased Almighty God, in His wise providence, to take out of this world the soul of our deceased brother, we therefore commit his body to the ground; earth to earth, ashes to ashes, dust to dust; looking for the general Resurrection in the last day, and the life of the world to come, through our Lord Jesus Christ."

At a nod from the preacher the widow dropped a handful of dirt onto the coffin, then, one by one, the other mourners filed by the open grave for a final good-bye. As the procession ended and the mourners left the graveyard, Dan moved down to talk to the widow. She had delayed her own departure as if, by that action, she could keep her husband with her a bit longer. Dan took off his hat and cleared his throat. The widow turned to look at him.

"Mrs. McGinnis, I want to tell you how sorry I am about what happened to your husband," he said.

Mrs. McGinnis wiped a tear from her cheek. "Were you a friend of my husband? I don't believe I've met you."

"I knew your husband," Dan said. "And we always had a friendly greeting for one another, though I wouldn't exactly say we were friends. My name is Efrem, ma'am. Dan Efrem. I'm the marshal over at Barlow."

"I see."

"I just wanted to let you know that I'm going after the man who did this. I'm going after Rufus Blanton and I'm going to bring him in."

"Is that supposed to comfort me, Marshal?"

Dan was a little surprised by the widow's reaction.

"Well I, uh, was hopin' you'd take some comfort in it, yes ma'am," he stammered.

"Why?"

"Well, if for no other reason, then to honor your husband's memory. He was a courageous man."

"Yes, everyone keeps telling me what a brave man he was," Mrs. McGinnis said. "They told me all about how he grabbed the shotgun and tried to shoot the robber."

"Yes, ma'am," Dan said. "There's not many men who would have had the courage to do that."

"The courage or the stupidity?" the widow asked.

"I beg your pardon?" Dan asked, more surprised than ever.

"What my husband did was a foolish thing," Mrs. McGinnis said. "What difference could it possibly have made to Andy whether or not the robber stole that money? It wasn't Andy's money. It wasn't even the stageline's money. It belonged to the Risco bank and they hardly even noticed it was gone. They opened up for business the next day same as always. Andy got himself killed, and for what? I take no comfort in the fact that he died bravely… or foolishly. Nor do I take comfort in the fact that you're going after the man who killed him. Will that bring Andy back?"

"No, ma'am, I don't suppose it will," Dan admitted.

"I'm confused about something anyway, Marshal. My husband lived in Risco and he was killed in the county where neither you nor the sheriff of Risco has any authority. Why are you so interested in going after Rufus Blanton? The sheriff of Risco certainly isn't."

"Rufus Blanton killed one of my closest friends some time back. I've got a score to settle with him for that."

"Then go after him if you must," Mrs. McGinnis said. "Just don't try and convince me that you are doing it for me."

Mrs. McGinnis turned back to face the grave. By now the grave digger was beginning to close the hole, and the ringing sound of dirt leaving the shovel blade was followed almost immediately by the sound of soil, landing on the freshly made pine coffin.

"No ma'am, I won't do that. I just wanted to tell you how sorry I am about your husband, that's all," Dan said, not quite sure how to handle the situation. Finally he decided to leave her alone to deal with her grief the best way she could.

A short while later in the Risco saloon, the mood was completely changed. One would hardly know that there had been a funeral, for the piano was playing merrily, glasses were clinking cheerily, laughter ebbed, and conversation flowed like water from table to table. When Dan stepped up and slapped a nickel on the bar, the sheriff of Risco sidled up toward him, smiling broadly.

"Put your nickel away, Dan," the sheriff said. "It's no good in this bar."

"Thanks, Pat," Dan said. He blew the foam off the beer the bartender served him, then took a long, Adam's apple-bobbing drink. "Ahhh," he said. "That was good."

"So, you've set out after Rufus Blanton, have you?" Pat asked.

Dan wiped his mustache off with the back of his hand.

"Yes."

Pat sighed. "I can't say as I envy you," he said. "As far as I'm concerned, ol' Ruthless can do all the mischief he wants outside the town limits. I'm just hopin' and prayin' he don't take a notion to come into town. 'Cause as long as he stays where he is, then he's none of my worry."

"What if everybody thought like that?"

"If more people thought like that there'd be more people stayin' alive," Pat answered.

Dan didn't respond to Pat's comment. Instead, he just took another swallow of beer.

"Are you that set about goin' out after him?" Pat finally asked.

"Yes."

Pat sighed. "I probably shouldn't tell you this," he said. "I mean, I think you'd be better off leavin' it alone. But if you're hell-bent to find him, you might want to have a look around over in Bragg City."

"Is Ruthless there?"

"According to a drummer who come into my office this morning, he is."

"Thanks," Dan said, draining the rest of his beer. "I guess I'll get over there and take a look around. In the meantime, you could do me a favor by wiring the sheriff of Bragg City and asking him to keep an eye on him for me."

Pat laughed. "You know who's sheriffin' over there?"

"Corey Summers, isn't it?"

Pat shook his head. "Not no more, he ain't. He's retired. Thurman Burnside's wearin' the badge."

"Thurman Burnside? He the one used to be the jailer up in San Angelo?"

"Same one. He's worthless as teats on a boar hog. If you recall, he once let ever'one in his jail escape 'cause he was frightened by a gun someone carved out of a piece of wood. If I was to even mention Ruthless's name in a telegram to him, it would probably scare him to death."

"All I want him to do is keep an eye on him and if he leaves, find out which way he went."

"Are you kidding?" the Western Union operator asked, when Dan inquired if the sheriff received the wire. "Why do you think Burnside's gone? He took one look at the telegram, then suddenly remembered an important piece of business he had to do somewhere else."

"Well, what about Ruthless? Is he still here?" The telegraph operator nodded. "He's here all right. You'll find him just down the street in the Bucket of Blood Saloon," he said. "He's been in there ever since he arrived, spendin' money like it was water and braggin' as to how he'd recently come into some good fortune."

"Good fortune, my ass. He robbed the Risco stage," Dan said. "Didn't you folks hear about that over here?"

"Oh, yeah, we heard about it. But I guess people around here figure the Risco stage ain't none of our business," the telegraph operator replied. He smiled. "Besides which, ol' Ruthless is spreadin' money around pretty good right now. He's bought a new saddle and some new duds, he's been eatin' fine in all the local cafes, and right now he's buyin' drinks for everyone down at the Bucket of Blood. He's just been real good for the town's business."

"Well, I hate to spoil everyone's good time, but I'm going to take Mr. Rufus 'Ruthless' Blanton to jail," Dan said. He loosened his pistol in his holster, then started toward the Bucket of Blood saloon.

"Marshal?" the telegraph operator called after him as he walked away.

Dan turned to look back. "Yeah?"

"You got anyone you want notified?"

"Notified?"

"I mean, if things don't go right for you?"

"You've got me dead already, have you?"

"They say he's faster'n greased lightning," the telegrapher replied. "You never know."

"No, I guess not. But, to answer your question, when I went into this business a long time ago I made it a point not to have anyone around that might mourn for me. No, there's no one."

"What about your deputy back in Barlow?" Dan thought for a moment before he answered, then he nodded his head affirmatively. "Lance Chaney, yes. I guess he would have to know. You could tell him, if it doesn't work out the way it should."

"I'll take care of it," the telegrapher promised solemnly.

By the time Dan Efrem reached the front of the saloon, everyone in town knew why he was here. His progress was the subject of close scrutiny from half a dozen or more of the town's more curious citizens. In the barbershop across the street the barber, his razor in his hand, stood at the window and watched. The barber's customer, wearing the protective apron and with the lower half of his face still lathered, got up from his chair to see for himself. On the second floor of the hotel next door to the saloon, a curtain moved slightly as someone peered around it. Down the street in the general store a young boy sucked on a piece of horehound candy as he knelt on a bolt of cloth and stared through the store name painted on the window at the marshal who had come to arrest Rufus Blanton.

Dan stopped in front of the saloon and composed himself for the task ahead. He could hear a sign creaking in the wind and flies buzzing loudly around a pile of horse manure. These sounds were magnified because the street had grown absolutely silent. Dan thought that was odd enough, it being the middle of the day, but what was even odder was that the saloon itself was quiet.

A moment later the silence was interrupted by the sound of footfalls on the broad-board saloon floor, then the squeak of the bat wing doors being pushed open from inside. They swung out over the saloon porch and a short, slender man, wearing a black hat with a silver band and a red feather, stepped outside. He looked toward Dan with his cold, flat, eyes and smiled. The smile was twisted and cheerless.

"Well, now, if it isn't my old friend, Marshal Dan Efrem," he said. "What brings you here, Marshal?"

"You know why I'm here, Ruthless. I'm here to take you in," Dan said.

Ruthless was sucking on a toothpick and he pulled it out of his mouth and examined the end of it for a moment.

"And if I don't want to go?"

"As I see it, you don't have much of a choice," Dan said. "I'm takin' you with me, whether you want to go or not."

"Is that a fact, now?"

"It purely is," Dan answered.

Ruthless flipped his toothpick away, and his smile became harder, then froze.

"Let's get this over with," he growled. Suddenly his hand dipped to his gun.

Ruthless was fast, so fast that even before Dan's hand wrapped around his own gun, he knew that he had already lost. In the brief instant that was left of his life, Dan felt surprise, panic, and then resignation. Once loosed, however, his reflexes continued the draw, and his gun was out and firing in one smooth operation, the discharge coming right on top of Ruthless' shot, though just a fraction of a second too late.

The ball from Ruthless' pistol had caught Dan heart-high and he was already dying even as he pulled the trigger for his own shot. He lived just long enough to see his bullet smack harmlessly into the boardwalk between Rufus Blanton's feet. By the time his forehead cracked against the edge of the saloon porch, Marshal Dan Efrem was dead.

CHAPTER 7

TRUE TO HIS WORD, THE TELEGRAPHER IN Bragg City sent a message to Deputy Marshal Lance Chaney, informing him that Marshal Dan Efrem had been killed. From the moment the instrument in Barlow began clacking, word spread through the little town. By the time the message was actually delivered to Lance, everyone else already knew about it.

Lily Montgomery showed up at the marshal's office within moments after the message had been delivered. Her face was drawn and worried.

"Lance, is it true what everyone is saying down in the Easy Pickin's? Has Dan Efrem really been killed?"

"I'm afraid so," Lance replied. Lance was looking through the drawers in Dan's desk, jerking one open, rummaging through its contents, then slamming it shut only to jerk open another.

Lily pushed a strand of hair back from her forehead. "Oh," she said. "Oh, how awful. Does he have a family? Is there anyone who should be notified?"

"I think he once told me he had a sister somewhere," Lance said, looking up from one of the drawers. "He didn't know exactly where, and he couldn't remember who she married, so he didn't even know her name."

"That means there would be no way of finding her," Lily said.

"No, I'm afraid not," Lance replied. "Ah, good, this is what I was looking for." He took out a badge and lay it on the desk.

"What do you want with that?"

"The town council is going to have to appoint a new deputy to look after things while I'm gone."

"While you're gone? What do you mean, while you're gone? Where are you going?"

"Where do you think he's goin', Missy?" Lattimore asked from his cell. He laughed, obscenely. "He's runnin' away, with his tail tucked between his legs. That's where he's goin'."

Lance took a rifle down from the rack and began loading it. "You know where I'm going, Lily. Where I have to go. I'm going after Rufus Blanton."

"Lance, no!" Lily gasped. "Rufus Blanton is not your responsibility."

"Then whose responsibility is he?"

"He's...he's..." Lily stammered, then, with an

exasperated sigh she admitted, "I don't know. But I know he isn't yours. Let it alone. Let someone else handle it."

"You better listen to the girly, Deputy." Lattimore said. "I know Rufus Blanton. He'll have you for breakfast." Again, Lattimore laughed.

"You're using the same argument on me that I tried to use on Dan," Lance said, ignoring Lattimore's comments as if the prisoner wasn't even present. "And it didn't work on him, either."

"Yes, and look where it got him. Lance, please don't do this. I'm afraid for you."

Lance chuckled. "Well, that makes two of us," he said. "I'm afraid for me too."

"Deputy?" someone called from the door, and when Lance looked up he saw that the telegraph operator had returned. "You're a popular man, today. I've got another message for you from Bragg City. This one is from Sheriff Burnside."

"He's probably wanting to know what to do with Dan's body," Lance said. "Tell him to send it here."

"No, that's not it," the telegrapher said. He held the message toward Lance. "I'd feel a lot better if that was all there was to it."

Puzzled by the telegrapher's strange comment, Lance took the little sheet of paper and read the message. Then he looked up at Lily with a wan smile. "I guess you win, Lily. I won't be going out after Mr. Blanton after all."

"Thank heaven you've finally got a little sense," Lily said. Then, seeing the expression on the telegrapher's face, she realized that there was more to it than Lance merely changing his mind. "Why aren't you going after him?" she asked.

"Because he's coming here," Lance said. He showed her the message from Sheriff Burnside. Rufus Blanton is heading for Barlow. Says he aims to make it an open town.

"Lance, leave town," Lily said.

Lance laughed out loud. "Come on, Lily, make up your mind, will you? A few moments ago you were wanting me to stay. Now you're wanting me to go."

"Yes," Lily said.

"You read the message, same as I did. Rufus Blanton is planning on making Barlow an open town. That sort of makes him my responsibility now, don't you think? I'm sure the town council would think so."

"Oh, hang the town council," Lily said. "You aren't the marshal. You're just a deputy."

"Not a deputy, Lily. The deputy," Lance said. "The only deputy, in a town that no longer has a marshal."

"Then if you aren't going to leave, at least go to the town council and have them appoint some more deputies to help you," Lily said.

"Say, she's got a point there, Deputy. That might

work," the telegrapher agreed. "Maybe if we had three or four deputies facing Rufus Blanton when he rode into town he'd take the hint and leave."

"Oh, I don't want him to leave," Lance said.

"What do you mean you don't want him to leave?" Lily asked.

"I want to see the man hanged. Now, whether I go out after him, or sit here and wait for him to come to me, it doesn't matter. I'm going to arrest him." He smiled. "But, I will take your advice on one thing," he said. "I will go to the town council and ask them to appoint a couple of deputies to help me."

"Oh, my. What a concession," Lily said in exasperated sarcasm.

Mayor Cravens, who was also the editor of the Barlow Vindicator, held the special meeting of the town council in the back of the newspaper office, just behind his brand new Washington Hand Press. Councilman Bixby let fly a quid of tobacco that made the spittoon ring, while Councilman Wallace busied himself with filling his pipe. Councilman Poindexter, who owned the emporium, was pacing back and forth, taking several trips to the window and looking out onto the street. He was anxious for the meeting to end because he was getting a wagonload of goods today and he felt it was necessary to witness the unloading to make sure he wasn't being cheated.

"The motion has been made that we appoint three temporary deputies to help Acting Marshal Chaney," Mayor Cravens said. "Second?"

"I second," Bixby said.

"All in favor, say aye."

"Aye," they all said as one.

"Motion is carried," the mayor said. "All right, Lance, you've got your authority. All you have to do now, is go out and find them."

Lance smiled. "Yeah," he said. "I was afraid it would come down to that. Any of you men got any ideas?"

"How about McPheeters?" Mayor Cravens suggested. "He's pretty much of a hell raiser. Seems like his name is in my paper all the time for getting into fights and such."

"I don't want someone who is a hell raiser," Lance said. "I want someone who is dependable."

"How about your brother?"

"I'm trying to find him now," Lance said. "I've sent telegrams out to every town within two hundred miles of here. He'll come, but the problem is he may not get here in time. If Ruthless is coming here from Bragg City, he'll be here by tomorrow morning, sure, tonight if he pushes it."

"How about Lucas Dolan? He was in the war."

"Yes, and he's still carrying a bullet in his leg to show for it. Besides which, he's got a wife and three kids," Lance said. "No, I'd rather have someone who won't be worrying about his family."

"Hell, give me one of the badges," Bixby said. "I'll help you."

"Thank you, Joe," Lance said. "But have you ever even fired a gun before?"

"No," the leather-worker admitted. "But other than pulling the trigger, what is there to shooting one of the damn things?"

"I appreciate your offer, Joe, I really do," Lance said. "But I don't think someone who is called 'Ruthless' is the kind of man you learn on."

"What about Farnsworth?" someone suggested, and someone went to get the young freight-wagon driver, only to find that he was out of town and would be gone for several days. One by one possibilities were discussed and eliminated, sometimes for valid reasons, sometimes because the candidates themselves refused. By the end of the day an indisputable pattern had emerged. Though the town council had authorized additional deputies, Lance Chaney was not going to be able to find anyone to help him. When Rufus Blanton arrived, Lance was going to have to face him alone.

"Suppose we just called a general town alert," Sam suggested late that night after a full day of fruitless searching. He was behind the bar wiping glasses. Lance was nursing a beer.

"What do you mean?"

"Well, I mean, what if we was going to be attacked by Indians or something? You think ever'one in town would just sit back and let the marshal do their fightin' for them?" Sam asked. "Hell no, they wouldn't. Why, we'd have wagon barricades drawn across the street, we'd have people posted on the roofs and behind buildings, and we'd turn this town into a fort."

"And that's what you suggest we do with Rufus Blanton?" Lance asked.

"Sure. Why not? We could all be waiting for him first thing in the morning, and shoot the sonofabitch as soon as he shows up."

"Ambush him, you mean?"

"Yeah," Sam said.

"No," Lance said, shaking his head. "That wouldn't be any different from a lynch mob."

"So what? Hell, if there was ever anybody who should be strung up from the nearest tree, it's Rufus Blanton."

"You got any particular tree in mind, barkeep?" someone asked from the far end of the bar. The stranger had come in a moment earlier, quiet and unobserved, and now he stood at the end, leaning on the bar with his hands clasped before him, almost as if in prayer.

"Sorry, stranger, didn't see you come in," Sam

said, starting toward him. "What'll it be? We got..." he stopped in midsentence. "My God," he gasped.

Lance, hearing Sam's gasp, glanced down the bar toward the stranger. Though Lance had never seen Rufus Blanton, he had heard him described... especially the black hat and the silver band with the red feather. This man fit that description.

"You would be Rufus Blanton?" Lance asked.

"That's right, Mister," Ruthless answered. "And who might you be?"

"Lance Chaney." Lance turned to face Ruthless. "Deputy Marshal Lance Chaney," he added.

By now, even those people in the most remote corners of the saloon realized that Rufus Blanton had just arrived and he and Lance Chaney were already confronting each other. The customers began scurrying, pushing tables aside and knocking over chairs in their haste to get out of the way.

"You put one over on us, Ruthless," Lance said. "We weren't looking for you 'til morning."

"So I gathered," Ruthless said, smiling a crooked, evil smile. "But, I kind of like to surprise people now and again. So, you're the deputy, are you?"

"That's right."

"Then I reckon that means you'll be workin' for me."

"Working for you?"

"Sure," Ruthless said. He pulled his vest to one

side and Lance recognized Dan's badge. "You see, when I killed the marshal of this town, I figured you fellas would be needin' a replacement, so I sort of appointed myself."

"Mister, that badge belonged to a good man," Lance said coldly. "You're not worthy to even look at it, much less wear it. Take it off."

"I'm touched by your loyalty," Ruthless said, sarcastically. "As your new marshal, I hope I can count on the same degree of loyalty from you."

"I said, take it off, you sawed-off, runty little sonofabitch," Lance said, making his hands into fists. "Or so help me, I'll take it off and ram it down your throat."

"Mister, that's brave talk from a muscle-bound bigmouth," Ruthless said. He stepped away from the bar and let his arms dangle by his side, his right hand open, his fingers flexing easily. "Tell me just how you plan to do all that after I kill you?"

"If I have to, I'll come back from hell," Lance said menacingly.

At that precise moment Lance saw something in Ruthless's eyes. Where before Ruthless had been confident to the point of contemptuousness, there now appeared a tiny flicker of fear. It went away as quickly as it came, but Lance was surprised to have seen it at all. He wondered what caused it, and more importantly, if it was something he could play to his advantage. His wondering didn't last very long, however, because he suddenly realized that Ruthless was about to draw, and he had no more time for contemplation.

Because Lance had been able to read it in Ruthless' eyes, he was able to start for his own pistol a split second before Ruthless. And, unlike many of Rufus Blanton's previous victims, Lance had faced death often enough to have control over his fear. He had everything in his favor when the two men started to draw...except speed.

Ruthless was fast, incredibly fast, and his gun was already firing as he brought it up and into position. His bullet hit Lance in the chest with the impact of a kicking mule. Lance tried to pull the trigger to return fire but when Ruthless' bullet hit him, the entire upper half of his body went instantly numb. He sent the message to his trigger finger to fire, but his trigger finger was quite unable to react.

The impact of the bullet slammed Lance back against the edge of the bar. He hit it, then slid down to the floor in a sitting position. Sam hurried around from the bar toward him, and, dimly, Lance heard someone shouting his name. Sounds seemed to come to him from far down in a cave and, though he knew they were talking about him, it was almost as if they were in another room, talking about someone else, and he was a distant and disinterested listener.

There were heavy footfalls on the boardwalk out front and several people came rushing through the bat wing doors to see what the shooting was about. One of the men was carrying a doctor's bag. Lance saw him coming toward him, then his vision dimmed, and finally went black.

"Doc Presnell," Sam said. "It's Lance."

"Let me have a look," Presnell said, kneeling down beside him.

"Lance! Oh, no, Lance!" a woman screamed, and everyone in the saloon looked toward the stairs where Lily, who had already retired for the night, now stood, looking down in horror at the men kneeling around the inert figure of Lance Chaney.

"Let's get him laid out," Doc Presnell said, and he and Sam stretched Lance out upon the floor.

"Is he dead?" Sam asked, anxiously.

"Oh, Doc, no. He's still alive, isn't he? You can save him, can't you?" Lily pleaded.

Doc Presnell put his hand on Lance's neck and held it there for a moment, then he sighed and shook his head, slowly.

"I'm sorry, Miss Lily," he said. "Lance is dead."

Ruthless walked around behind the bar and took a bottle of whiskey from the shelf, then poured himself a drink.

"You know, you folks didn't really need a doctor to tell you that," Ruthless said easily. "I could have told you he was dead from the moment I pulled the trigger."

"You…you bastard!" Lily screamed, and she started toward him.

Ruthless pulled his pistol and fired into the ceiling. The sudden, unexpected thunderclap of another gunshot stopped Lily's charge, and Ruthless lowered his pistol and pointed it at her.

"You'd better stop right there, lady," he said. "If you think I won't shoot you just because you're a woman, then you've got yourself another think comin'. Killin' is killin'. It's what I do and I'm pretty damned good at my work."

"Yes," Doc Presnell said. "I've examined a couple examples of your handiwork over the last few days. The stage driver and this man."

"Then you know I ain't playin' around," Ruthless said, menacingly.

"Back away from him, Miss Lily, please," Sam begged.

"You'd better listen to the barkeep, lady," Ruthless said.

Lily turned away from him and put her hands to her eyes. She was sobbing out loud.

"Couple of you fellas take that door down," Doc said, pointing to the door that opened into the kitchen. "Let's put the deputy on it and get him down to Albritton's Funeral Parlor. Miss Lily, you want to come along with us?"

"Oh, Doc, I don't know," Lily said between sobs. "I don't know if I can stand it."

The door was taken down and Lance was moved, carefully, onto it.

"We're ready," one of the men said.

"All right, let's get him down there," Doc Presnell said. He looked over at Lily again. "Please come along with us, Miss Lily. I think Lance would like it, you making this last walk with him."

"Oh, God," Lily cried. "I can't believe he's gone. Buck," she suddenly said. "Someone is going to have to get word to Buck. He'll need to know about this."

"We'll get word to him, Miss Lily, I promise," Sam said as she, Doc Presnell, and the sad little party left the saloon.

Those who had moved out of the way during the shooting now began to return, and tables and chairs were put back into position as they took their seats and resumed their activity. Conversation started again, but it was hushed and whispered.

***

"Barkeep," Ruthless said, as he poured himself another drink. "Who is this Buck they're talking about?"

"Buck Chaney," Sam said. "He's the deputy's

brother. Under the circumstances, I'd say he wasn't a person you want to meet."

"Well, now, that's just where you're wrong, Barkeep," Ruthless said. "You see, Mr. Buck Chaney and I have crossed paths before. And I'm lookin' forward to seein' him again."

"I recall that now," Sam said. "Accordin' to the newspapers, he killed two of your men and drove you off during an attempted train robbery."

"Train robbery? What train robbery?" Ruthless replied. "Don't believe everything you read in the newspapers. However, I am looking forward to facing Mr. Buck Chaney. We'll just see who the fastest man with a gun is.

"You say you plan to see who is the fastest?" Sam asked.

"Yes. Then we'll see what the newspapers have to say about the hero who stopped a train robbery."

Sam shook his head and chuckled. "You still don't understand, do you, Mr. Ruthless?"

"I don't understand what?"

"It doesn't matter who is the fastest."

"What do you mean it doesn't matter? It mattered with Marshal Efrem, didn't it? It mattered with Lance Chaney."

"The difference is, Buck doesn't care how things look. If he thinks you need killin' he'll kill you. He doesn't have to meet you in the middle of the street to do that. Hell, he'd just as soon kill you in your bed."

"Yeah? Well, we'll see just who kills who," Ruthless said. He poured himself another drink and Sam noticed, with some satisfaction, that this time he spilled a little.

CHAPTER 8

THE EASY PICKIN'S SALOON WAS CLOSED, so Ruthless went across the street to the Angry Bull. As the Angry Bull generally appealed to a somewhat rougher trade than the Easy Pickin's, its appointments weren't quite as nice. The bar was not finished off, the liquor selection was limited, and the rooms upstairs were available on an hourly basis, only.

There were four men playing cards at one of the tables inside the Angry Bull. One of the four was Titus Lattimore. Lattimore had not only been freed by Ruthless, he had also been made a deputy.

"Where the hell is ever'body?" Ruthless asked, as he stepped up to the bar. The bartender moved down to him and took a bottle from under the bar. Unlike the bottles on the shelves behind the bar, this one had a label, indicating it was a better stock than that normally served to the Angry Bull customers.

That the bartender served Ruthless bonded whiskey without specifically being asked to do so, was an indication of how frightened of Rufus he was.

"Why, they're all at Deputy Chaney's funeral," the bartender said, as he poured the glass. "The whole town is closed up…stores, shops, the bank, even the other saloons."

"Yeah?" Ruthless said. He tossed down the drink then wiped his mouth with the back of his hand and slid the glass out for a second. "How come you ain't?"

"You won't find me sheddin' no tears over Deputy Chaney," the bartender said, pouring a second glass. He pointed to the table of card players. "Nor any of them gents, either."

"Say, Ruthless, how 'bout we make these fellas deputies, too?" Lattimore called from the table.

"Sure," Ruthless replied. "Why not?" He took his glass and walked over to stand at the bat wing doors and look out onto the street. Down at the far end of the street, stood a little white church. There were dozens of carriages and wagons tied up in front of the church, though the most prominent vehicle was the black, glass-sided hearse. It stood under the shade of a tree, waiting for its cargo.

"Don't you want to know their names?" Lattimore asked.

"Yeah, sure," Ruthless answered over his shoulder, though he continued to stare at the little white church at the end of the street.

"The big'un here, is Deke Wooley. The one with the scar on his face is Ramsey Jones, and the other is Red Smith." Lattimore chuckled. "Lookin' at his hair and them freckles, I reckon you know why they call him Red."

The church bell began to peal.

"What are they ringin' that bell for?" Ruthless asked, showing no sign that he even heard the names.

"Why, they got to," the bartender replied. "What do you mean, they got to?"

"Ain't you ever heard? You got to ring the bell exactly the same number of times as the number of years the dead person lived. Otherwise, his soul is lost in limbo."

"Lost in limbo? What does that mean?"

"It means the soul don't go to Heaven or Hell. It just wanders around."

"You mean like a ghost?" Red Smith asked. "Yeah, sort of like that, I suppose," the bartender answered.

"Ooooooohhh. I'm the ghost of Deputy Chaney," Red said, and the others laughed.

"Shut up!" Ruthless said, turning away from the door and pointing at the men sitting at the table. "All of you. Just shut the hell up!"

"Hey, come on, Ruthless, we didn't mean nothin'

by it," Lattimore said. "The boys was just havin' a little fun, that's all."

"Yeah? Well, anymore fun like that and I'll turn one of you into a real ghost, if you get my meanin'," Ruthless said, menacingly.

"We get your meanin'," Deke Wooley said. Ruthless turned back toward the church and saw that the front doors had been thrown open. Six men came through the door, carrying a coffin. Gingerly, they slid the coffin into the back of the hearse. Others began pouring out of the church then, and, within a few moments, a procession was formed. With the hearse leading the way, the funeral cortege started down the street, heading slowly and somberly toward Boothill, the cemetery at the opposite end of town. Some of the mourners rode in carriages or wagons, though just as many walked.

"Get over here," Ruthless said gruffly. "All of you. Get over here and show some respect for the dead." Ruthless took off his hat.

"Ruthless, you can't be serious," Lattimore said. "You're the one that killed the sonofabitch."

"I'm very serious," Ruthless said coldly.

With a shrug of his shoulders, Lattimore looked at the other men who were sitting around the table with him, then, to a man, they rose and walked over to the front door. Ruthless moved out onto the porch and indicated that they should do the same.

Then, as the funeral cortege passed by, Ruthless and his newly appointed corps of "deputies" stood by silently, with their heads bared.

Lily Montgomery, dressed in black, and wearing a long, black veil, rode in the first buggy behind the hearse. The buggy was being driven by Sam Goodbody. When Lily saw Ruthless and the others making a gesture of respect she looked, pointedly, away from them.

"Did you see what they carved onto the grave marker?" Deke asked.

"Where'd you see the grave marker?"

"When I come by the undertaker's place a while ago, it was outside, leanin' against the front wall."

"What'd it say?"

"It said, 'Here lies Lance Chaney, murdered by Ruthless Blanton.'"

"If you want, Ruthless, I'll go down there and make 'em change it," Lattimore offered.

"No," Ruthless said. "No, hell no, leave it alone. I like it."

"You like it?"

"Hell yes. Don't you see? People will read that and they'll know I'm not a man to cross."

"Yeah," Lattimore said. He laughed. "Yeah, I guess you're right."

"Now that we paid our respect, are we goin' down to the buryin'?" Deke wanted to know.

"No," Ruthless replied. "He's dead, he ain't goin' to be no problem now."

"What about Buck Chaney?" Ramsey asked.

"What about him?" Ruthless replied.

"He's goin' to be comin' after you, soon as he finds out what happened last night."

"Yes, I suppose he will," Ruthless replied.

"He don't have to, you know," Ramsey suggested. "What do you mean?"

"I mean, it don't have to come to that. If you'd like, Deke, Red and me can take care of him for you. We could ride out and find him, and take care of the situation before he ever even got here."

Ruthless studied the three men as he stroked his chin. "Yeah," he said. "Yeah, that might not be a bad idea. I mean, once he hears about his brother, he's goin' to want to be comin' after me, so he won't have his mind on anything else. You could probably get a really good crack at him before he even knows you're around. That is, if you're willin' to do it."

"Oh, we're willin', all right," Angus replied. "It's the least we can do for you makin' us deputies. And I figure bein' a deputy in a wide-open town like this, is goin' to be real good."

Ruthless smiled. "Yeah," he said. "Yeah, you're right. All right, hold up your right hands," he ordered, and all three men did as they were instructed. "Do you swear to do whatever I tell you to do?"

"Yeah," the men replied, grinning at each other. "You're deputies," Ruthless said easily. "Now, go take care of Buck Chaney for me."

"Red, you know him pretty good don't you?" Deke asked.

"Well, we ain't exactly pards, if that's what you mean," Red replied. "But I've played cards with him a few times."

"You got any idea where we might find him?"

"Not just off hand. But, he's a slick gambler, and a ladies' man," Red replied. "How hard can he be to find?"

Sam Goodbody stopped the buggy in front of the Easy Pickin's Saloon, then helped Lily down.

"Will you be openin' up any today, Miss Lily?" Sam asked.

"No," Lily replied. "Put a black wreath up on the door. And hang up a sign, telling folks we'll be closed for three days."

"Yes, ma'am," Sam said.

"Oh, and tell all the girls they can have off a week, with pay," Lily said. "There's no sense in them staying around while we're closed."

***

"Yes, ma'am. I 'spect they'll appreciate that," Sam said.

Lily walked through the quiet bar area of the saloon. It was lighted by splashes of sunlight which managed to find its way in through the cracks and gaps of the closed window shutters. Lily pulled the hat pin from her stiffened hat and took it and the veil off, wadding the little bits of cloth and stiffener in her hands as she climbed the stairs to the top floor. When she reached the top of the stairs she looked down toward the closed door of Lance's room, sighed, then moved quickly down the hall to her own room.

"How did the funeral go?" Doc Presnell asked, when Lily let herself in.

"It went fine," Lily said.

"Anybody say anything about my not being there?"

"Not that I overheard," Lily said. "Maybe no one even noticed. The funeral was well attended. Nearly everybody in town was there."

"Well, of course it would be. Lance was a very popular man. Did you expect it to be any different?" Doc Presnell asked.

"No, no, I was sure there would be a crowd. It's just that, well, Doc, I don't know. I feel like we're being dishonest with all these people."

"Maybe we are," Doc said. "But we can't afford to let anyone know what's going on. At least, not yet. And when the people find out what we did and why we did it, they'll forgive us. Believe me, Lily, they will forgive us."

"I suppose so. How is the patient doing?"

"He's sleeping," Doc Presnell said. "You want to look in on him?"

"Yes," Lily said. She walked over to her bedroom and looked inside. There, on the bed, his chest swathed in bandages and his eyes closed in troubled sleep, lay Lance Chaney. "Is he going to make it, Doc?"

"I wish I could say yes and be for certain," Doc Presnell said. "He survived the first twenty-four hours and that's good. Every day he stays alive is one day of getting stronger."

"But you said none of the vital organs were hit."

"That's true. But he did lose a lot of blood. And there's still a danger of infection. I'm sorry, Lily. I wish I could be more encouraging."

"Don't apologize, Doc," Lily said. "He's alive now, because of you. Not only because of your doctoring, but also because of your quick wit. Who would have thought to pronounce him dead so that Ruthless wouldn't shoot him again?"

"Yes, well, Ruthless still might come around if he finds out what he did. That's why I have to keep him over here. I can't take a chance on keeping him in my office."

"Here's fine," Lily said. "I can't think of anyplace

I would rather him be."

"I'm going to have to depend on you to take care of all the nursing," Doc Presnell said. "You're going to have to keep his bandages changed, keep him clean and warm. It's going to take a lot of hard work and prayer."

"Hard work and prayer I can provide, Doc. And plenty of it, too," Lily promised.

Doc Presnell reached out and patted Lily on the hand. "I know you will, Lily," he said. "As far as I'm concerned, Lance wouldn't have any better chance if he was in the finest hospital in the world. Now, I've got to get back over to see to Seth. He was runnin' some fever earlier today. I've got to make sure there's no infection gettin' started anywhere. I'll drop back in tomorrow."

"All right, Doc," Lily said. "And thanks. Thanks for everything."

After Doc Presnell left, Lily pulled up a rocking chair and sat next to Lance's bed. She rocked back and forth, slowly, all the while looking into Lance's face. It was a nice face. There may be faces more handsome, but none more pleasing to her eyes.

Lance's eyes were closed now, but she wished they were open. His eyes were the most fascinating feature about his face. They were deep and dark and when she looked into them long enough and hard enough, she would sometimes feel herself spinning away into dizziness, like trying to contemplate eternity.

"Lance," she said, softly. "Lance, I know you can't hear me now, but I want to tell you that I'm not going to let you die. Do you hear me? I am not going to let you die!"

Lily raised up in her chair a little to see if her words had had any effect on Lance. It didn't appear that they had.

"I sent telegrams out today to find Buck," she went on. "I don't have any idea where he is, so I told the telegrapher to just send them out to every town within a hundred and fifty miles of here that has a telegraph operator. The only thing...and I hated to do this but Buck will understand why, when he gets here...I had to say that you and Dan had both been killed. It's going to be rough on him when he first hears." Suddenly, and inexplicably, she smiled. "But then, when he learns that you aren't dead, he'll be as happy as I was. And it was almost worth the despair to have that joy."

Like Lance's room, Lily's was on the front, facing the street. Lily's room, however, was at one end of the building, while Lance's room was at the other. From the Angry Bull Saloon across the street, Lily heard a gunshot, then a crash of glass, and finally, a loud peal of laughter. On the street just outside, there was a clatter of hoofbeats as several horses came thundering into town. One of the riders let out a whoop as he swung down from his mount.

"Wide open!" someone shouted, following the shout with a laughter. "We can come in off the plains, boys! We got us our own town."

Half a dozen more shots were fired, then a woman screamed in fear, and her scream was followed by more laughter.

"Buck will come, Lance, don't you worry," Lily said. "Buck will come, and he'll know what to do."

CHAPTER 9

TWO HUNDRED MILES SOUTHWEST OF Barlow, in the town of Carter City, Buck Chaney was enjoying a bath in the back room of the Silver Dollar Inn. His dirty clothes had already been given over to the operator of a Chinese laundry which was next door to the Silver Dollar. A clean pair of breeches and a fresh shirt hung over the back of a nearby chair. A cigar was elevated at a jaunty angle from Buck's freshly shaven face, and he was trying to wash his own back while at the same time singing "Buffalo Gals."

"What do you mean singing at this hour of the morning?" a woman asked, coming into the room. "Haven't you ever heard the old saying, "'Sing before breakfast, cry before supper?'"

"And what would I have to be crying about, Katie?" Buck wanted to know.

"I don't know. Maybe you'll have bad luck with

the cards." She took the back scrubber and began washing his back.

"Ahh," Buck said in contentment. "That's good, that's good. Now, a little lower and to the right, if you don't mind. Anyway, what if the cards did turn bad? Unlucky in cards, lucky in love. So, how can I possibly lose?"

"You are full of it, Buck Chaney. Where've you been keeping yourself? You haven't been in Carter City in two or three months," Katie asked.

"Oh, here, there, and around," Buck answered noncommittally. "Last place I was was Bitter Springs. I left it a few days ago…been on the trail since."

"You've got no business in Bitter Springs, anyway," the woman purred. "There ain't nobody over there that loves you like I do."

Buck laughed. "Don't you be pulling my leg now, Katie. You love anyone who can meet your price."

"That's true," Katie admitted. "But I love some more than others. And I love you most of all."

"I'm sure you do," Buck said. "By the way, I asked Tony to fix us some biscuits and gravy."

"You did, did you? Well, did you ever think to ask if I wanted biscuits and gravy? Maybe I'd rather have flapjacks."

"When you eat breakfast with me, you eat what I eat."

"And what if I don't want to eat breakfast with you?"

"That's all right. I'm sure there are plenty of girls around who would."

"Buck Chaney!" Katie said in an exasperated tone of voice. She swung the back-scrubbing brush at him, knocking his cigar out of his mouth.

The door opened then and Tony, the proprietor, came in. "Listen, if you folks are goin' to eat, you better come on out and get started. I got it all ready and gravy ain't no good once it gets cold."

"Gravy isn't any good when it's hot, either, so what difference does it make?" Katie asked, sullenly.

"By the way, you goin' to be much longer in here?" Tony asked. "I got another customer wantin' to use the water."

"I only want to use it if it doesn't get too dirty," a third voice said, stepping through the open door. He walked over to the tub and stuck his hand down into the water. "It's already getting pretty gamey, but I suppose it'll be all right if you get out now, before it gets too cold."

"Tony, I'm goin' to get some more bacon back out of the smokehouse," the cook said, coming in then. "I done used up what we brought in this morning."

"Damn it! Would somebody please tell me what the hell is going on around here?" Buck exploded, looking at the four people standing around his tub. "Is somebody selling tickets to this or what? Can't you folks see I'm taking a bath?"

"Hell yes, Mister, we can all see that," one of the breakfast customers shouted. The shout was followed by raucous laughter and Buck saw that by now the door was standing wide open, exposing him to anyone who might want to look.

"Get the hell out of here," Buck ordered, splashing water on all of them. "And close the damn door behind you. You," he added, looking pointedly at Katie. "Do you want to eat breakfast with me, or not?"

"Yes, of course."

"Then wait at my table. I'll be there shortly. And you," he added, looking at the man who wanted to use the bath water. "If you'll get out of here right now, I promise not to piss in the tub."

"I'm going, I'm going," the man sputtered, hurrying out with the others then closing the door on the laughter of the customers who had been privy to the exchange.

"What have you heard from your brother?" Katie asked a few minutes later as she sat across the breakfast table from Buck. She cut off a piece of gravy-covered biscuit and transferred it to her mouth.

"To be honest with you, it's been a couple of

months since I heard anything," Buck answered. "But, I was thinking I might ride over to Barlow after I spend a little time here, just to check on things."

"I hear he's sweet on Lily Montgomery."

"They're good friends," Buck admitted.

"More'n friends, I hear. I hear they're practically engaged."

"Is that a fact?"

"I think it's interesting, don't you? I mean that Lance Chaney who is so straight about everything else, could feel that way about a common saloon girl."

"I don't think my brother would like to hear you refer to Lily as a common saloon girl. In fact, I don't know that I like it. Lily Montgomery is anything but common. She happens to be one of the finest ladies I've ever known."

"Are you trying to tell me she isn't on the line like the rest of us?"

"That's exactly what I'm telling you," Buck replied. "Excuse me, sir," he said to a man at the table next to him. The man had just put down a newspaper. "Are you finished with that paper?"

"Yes, I am," the man said. "Would you care to read it?"

"Thank you," Buck said, accepting the offer. He began looking through it and chuckled at one of the advertisements. "Here is a new elixir that is guaranteed to cure everything from dropsy to baldness. My, my, what will science think of next?"

"I don't believe any of that stuff," Katie said.

Buck gasped in an exaggerated fashion. "What? You would dare scoff at the miracles wrought by men of science?"

"Yes, I would dare," Katie replied with a little laugh.

"Oh, shit, when did this happen?" Buck asked, suddenly growing very somber.

"What?" Katie wanted to know, curious as to why his sudden shift of mood.

"Dan Efrem has been killed," Buck answered. "It says here he was shot down by Rufus Blanton."

"Rufus Blanton? You mean the one they call Ruthless?" Katie asked.

"Yeah, I guess so. Damn, listen to this," Buck said, reading on. "According to witnesses, it was a fair fight. Blanton shot Dan Efrem down in a fair fight. I don't believe that."

"Why don't you believe it? Ruthless is supposed to be a very good gunfighter."

"Supposed to be," Buck replied. "There is no 'supposed to be' about Dan Efrem. He is very good. I know, because I've seen him in action."

"But you said it was a fair fight," Katie reminded him.

"No, I didn't say it. The newspaper said it." Buck stroked his chin. "That leaves my brother as the marshal now. I hope he doesn't get some fool notion in his head about going after Rufus Blanton."

"Do you think he will?"

"Yeah, I'm afraid so. He's real big on obligations and responsibility," Buck said. He put the newspaper down and began eating again. "Maybe I'd better start on back toward Barlow a little sooner than I'd planned. Lance is too proud to ask me, but I have a feeling he's going to need help."

"Excuse me, sir," a young boy said. He was wearing a hat which read Western Union. "Would you be Mr. Buck Chaney?"

"I'm guilty," Buck said, holding up his hands as if surrendering.

"I've got a telegram for you," the boy said, handing a little yellow envelope over to him.

"Thanks," Buck said, taking a nickel from his pocket and handing it to the boy.

"No, sir," the boy said, waving the nickel away. "I don't think it would be right, under the circumstances."

"What do you mean?"

"I'm sorry," the boy mumbled, then, he turned and walked quickly from the dining room.

"Buck, what is it?" Katie asked. "What did he mean by, 'under the circumstances?'"

"I don't know," Buck said. "But I'm about to find out." He read silently, then put his hand to his forehead. "Shit," he said, quietly.

Katie reached for the telegram which Buck sur-
rendered without protest.

Lance killed today by Rufus Blanton. Please return to Barlow
as quickly as possible.
Lily

"Are you going back?" Katie asked.

"Yes, of course."

"What if Rufus Blanton is still there?"

"All the more reason for me to go back."

"So you can fight him?"

"Yes."

"Why? It won't do your brother any good. He's
dead. And if you go up against Rufus Blanton, you
could be dead too."

"That's right."

"But you're going anyway, aren't you?"

"You're right again," Buck said. He tapped his lips
with a napkin, then stood up. "I'll see you, Katie."

"No!" Lance suddenly shouted, and he sat up in
bed and swung his legs over the edge so quickly that
Lily, who had been dozing in a rocking chair, was
caught unawares. "I've got to get to my men!" Lance
said. He tried to stand up.

"Lance! Lance, what are you doing?" Lily asked.
"You'll open up your wound. You'll start bleeding
again."

"Excuse me, ma'am," Lance said. He looked toward the door, then called out loud: "First Sergeant! First Sergeant, get in here!" Lance tried to stand up. "Where is my First Sergeant?" he asked.

"Lance! Lance, it's me, Lily! Don't you know me?"

Lance looked at Lily with eyes which were burning with intensity. "Lily? What are you doing here?" he asked. "You've got to get out of here! The battle is going to begin at any moment! The Rebels are massing their troops on the other side of the trees."

"Lance, listen to me," Lily said. "That war is over. Do you hear me? That war is over. You are safe now. You are here, in my bedroom."

"Your bedroom?" Lance asked, sitting back down on the edge of the bed. He put his hand over his wound, and it came away bloody. Lance looked around in confusion. "I am in your bedroom," he said. "What am I doing in here?"

"You've been shot," Lily said.

Lance looked down at his chest. "Yes," he said, dryly. "Well, I may not know what the hell is going on anywhere else, but I can tell I've been shot. It hurts like hell."

"Lay back down," Lily ordered. "I need to change the dressing now."

"All right," Lance said, obeying her order without question.

Lily poured some water into a basin and brought

it over to put on the little table beside the bed. Gingerly, she began removing his old bandage, then started bathing the wound.

"It was Rufus Blanton, wasn't it?" Lance asked.

"Yes."

"I remember now." Lance looked around Lily's bedroom as she continued to treat his wound. He smiled. "I guess I'd have done about anything to get in here," he teased. "But I didn't think I'd have to get shot to do it. What I want to know is, why am I in here, instead of down at the Doc's office?"

"Doc thought it would be best to keep you in here, out of sight," Lily said.

"Out of sight?"

"From Ruthless."

"Look here! Are you telling me I'm hiding from that bastard?" Lance asked angrily, trying again to sit up.

"Will you lie still?" Lily demanded, pushing him back down.

"Lily, I don't intend to skulk around, hiding, like some whipped pup," Lance said.

"Do you mean to say you'd rather go out there and get yourself killed?"

"I mean to say I don't intend to hide here, in your bedroom. My God, woman, don't you know what that makes me?"

"It makes you alive," Lily answered, "when Ruthless and the entire town think you are dead."

"They think I'm dead?"

"And buried," Lily said. She finished cleaning the wound, and now she began putting a fresh bandage on. "We had your funeral. There was quite a turn-out, too. You were a popular citizen of the town, Lance Chaney."

Despite the wound and the implications of "hiding out," Lance found something funny in the thought of a fake funeral, and he laughed.

"Was there much wailing and gnashing of teeth?" he asked.

"Oh yes," Lily replied, getting into the spirit of it with him. "Especially among the women. They cried bitter tears as if they had lost their one true love."

"And you, Lily Montgomery. Did you cry?"

"I cried the loudest," she said. She smiled at him. "Even though I knew you were here, safe, in my bed."

"And Ruthless? He really thinks I'm dead?"

"Doc pronounced you dead, right downstairs on the floor of the Easy Pickin's. So you see, Lance, you aren't really hiding from Ruthless, because he isn't looking for you."

"Where is he now?"

Almost as if in direct answer to his question, there were several gunshots fired out in the street, then a man's loud howl, followed by laughter.

"Does that answer your question?" Lily asked, nodding toward the window. "That sort of stuff has been going on day and night, ever since you got shot. Ruthless has put out the word that Barlow is an open town, and he is welcoming every thief, murderer, and outlaw in the state of Texas. The decent folks of Barlow are pretty much staying in their homes, going out only when it is absolutely necessary. A woman can't even walk down the street now, without fear of being accosted by one of the brigands who have responded to Ruthless' call."

"How long has this been going on?"

"Ever since you were shot."

"And how long has that been?"

"Four days."

"Four days? You mean I've been out for four days?" Lance asked.

"You've had periods when you were talking some," Lily said. "But I knew even then, that you wouldn't be remembering what you were saying. Especially when you believed you were back in the war."

"Who knows that I'm alive?"

"Just Doc, Sam Goodbody and me," Lily said. "What about Buck?"

"We've sent for him," Lily replied. "But I had to tell him in the telegram that you were dead. We couldn't let the word get out that you were still alive."

"If you can, you need to get to Buck before he goes off and does something foolish. You know what a hothead he is."

"Yes, well there is already something that will cool him off a little," Lily said. She walked over to the chest to pick up a piece of paper and bring it back to Lance. "Our new marshal," she twisted the word "marshal" showing her disdain, "had more than a thousand of these wanted posters printed. He's spread them all over."

"Damn!" Lance said. "Folks who see that and don't know that Rufus Blanton has taken over here, won't be able to tell the difference between that and a real dodger. Not only that, fifteen hundred dollars will get everyone who can carry a gun out to look for him."

"Do you think Ruthless really would pay fifteen hundred dollars for someone to kill Buck?"

"I seriously doubt it," Lance replied. "But it doesn't matter. The people who are out trying to collect the reward won't know that, any more than they know that the dodgers are phony."

"I just hope he gets here all right."

"Where is he now, do you know?"

"I sent telegrams out to more than two dozen towns. According to the telegrapher, one of them caught up with him in Carter City. That's nearly two hundred miles, so it's going to take him quite a while to get here."

"Yeah," Lance said. "But the good thing is, that's too far away for all the wanted posters. There may be a bounty hunter or two who'll go down there looking for him, but he shouldn't have to be afraid that some farmer or store clerk will shoot him in the back for the reward money."

"What frightens me," Lily said, "is that Buck has no idea Ruthless has put out a reward for him. He's in danger and he doesn't even know it." Lance chuckled. "Don't you worry about that," he said. "Buck is the kind of man that thrives on danger. He'll get through all right. I promise you that."

The handle of the coffeepot Buck had suspended over the open flames was so hot that he had to use his hat in order to pour himself a second cup of coffee. He was about to hang the pot up again when he sensed, rather than saw or heard, that someone was watching him. The hair on the back of his neck stood on end, and he forced himself to take a slow, deep breath, in order to remain calm.

"I got nearly a whole pot of coffee here, if you'd like some," he said, calmly.

There was a quiet chuckle from the dark, then Buck heard the sound of someone walking. A moment later a man appeared in the edge of the golden bubble of light cast from the small campfire.

"I guess I wasn't as quiet as I thought I was," the man said. He took a collapsible cup from his pocket and held it out. "I reckon I will have some coffee if you don't mind."

Buck poured the coffee and examined the man closely. The stranger had clear, blue eyes, a long, narrow face and a bushy beard. Buck had never seen him before.

"That's kind of dangerous isn't it?" Buck asked. "I mean, comin' up on a man's camp as quiet as all that."

The stranger took the cup and then squatted on his heels. He slurped a swallow of coffee through lips extended slightly to allow the coffee a chance to cool.

"I don't know, you might be right," the stranger admitted. "The truth is, I've never quite been able to figure out which way is best. Some folks are so nervous they'll just start banging away the moment they hear you, without even givin' you a chance to explain yourself. People like that, it's generally best for them to never even know you're in the area."

"Yeah," Buck said, still eyeing the stranger suspiciously. "But I'm not like that."

The stranger chuckled. "No, I reckon you ain't."

"So?" Buck asked. "Why are you here?"

"I'm a hunter," the man said.

"Not much game in these parts at this time of year," Buck said.

"Depends on what kind of game a fella might be huntin'," the stranger replied.

"I reckon it does," Buck agreed. Once again the hackles on the back of his neck stood up. "What kind of game are you after?"

"Men," the stranger said easily. "You see, I'm a bounty hunter."

Buck took another swallow of coffee and studied the stranger over the rim of his cup.

"I get it," he said. "It's the article in the paper about my run-in with Rufus Blanton, isn't it?" "Not exactly," the bounty hunter answered. "It's about someone else...someone whose name and picture is on a new wanted poster I came across. There's a fifteen hundred dollar reward for him."

"Fifteen hundred dollars? Damn, that's more than they've got out for Rufus Blanton," Buck said. "Who is this man?"

The stranger stood up and began reaching into his shirt pocket. "Here," he said. "I'll let you see for yourself." He tossed a folded-over piece of paper down toward Buck.

Buck unfolded the paper and looked at it.

WANTED, DEAD OR ALIVE
BUCK CHANEY

FIFTEEN HUNDRED DOLLARS
WILL BE PAID BY THE CITY MARSHAL OF
BARLOW, TEXAS UPON DELIVERY OF THE
PERSON OF BUCK CHANEY,
DEAD OR ALIVE

"Damn," Buck said, looking up in surprise. "That's..."

"You," the stranger said, easily. Buck's surprise was complete then, when he saw that the stranger was holding a gun pointed toward him.

"Mister, there's been a big mistake made here," Buck said. "I don't know what this is all about, but the marshal of Barlow is a friend of mine. And the deputy is my..." Buck paused in midsentence. He could no longer say that. Dan and his brother were both dead. He had no idea who the marshal of Barlow might be now. He sighed. "All right, if you need to take me in to get this all cleared up, I'll go with you. I'm on my way there, anyway."

The stranger's smile broadened, but there was nothing gentle about it.

"I'm afraid it don't work that way, Friend," the bounty hunter said.

"What do you mean?"

"I don't need your company, Mister. Just your carcass."

"You mean you're planning to shoot me?"

"You figured that out, did you?" the bounty

hunter asked. The smile left his face. "Talkin's over, Mister. You got five seconds to make your peace."

"Don't need to make my peace," Buck said. "All I need to do is finish my coffee."

"Go ahead," the bounty hunter said, generously. "Don't like to send a man to hell on an empty stomach."

"Mind if I warm it?" Buck asked, reaching for the pot with his left hand.

"Go ahead. Just don't get any fancy ideas about maybe tossing the coffee in my face," the bounty hunter said. "If I see that pot so much as wiggle in this direction, I'm shooting."

"Is that supposed to scare me?" Buck asked. "You already told me you're going to shoot me."

"Yeah, I guess I did at that."

"But don't worry. I'm not going to try and throw the pot at you or anything," Buck said. He began pouring coffee with his left hand and he poured too much so that it splashed down over the edge of the cup, running onto his hand.

"Damn!" Buck shouted out in pain, dropping the cup. At the same time his hand dipped to the pistol at his side, whipped it out, and then fired before the bounty hunter caught on to what he was doing. The bullet caught the bounty hunter right in the center of his chest, knocking him down before he could even pull the trigger.

Buck cocked his pistol for a second shot, but he saw immediately that a second shot wouldn't be needed.

"Damn!" the bounty hunter said with an expulsion of breath. "Damn! Damn, you got me good with that one. Where'd you learn a trick like that?"

"I don't know," Buck said. "It just came to me, I guess." Buck eased the hammer down on his pistol then knelt beside the wounded bounty hunter. He could see the blood frothing at the entry hole, and he knew his bullet had penetrated the lungs. He tore off a piece of the bounty hunter's shirt and stuck it in the hole to slow the bleeding, but he knew he was just wasting his time.

"No use in doin' all that," the bounty hunter said, indicating that he, too, knew it was a waste of time. "I could hear this wound suckin' air. Ain't never know'd anybody to survive a wound that sucks air. Have you?"

"No," Buck said easily.

The bounty hunter tried to chuckle, but the chuckle turned into a hacking cough. "Damn," he said. "You could'a lied to me...try to make me feel better."

"I reckon I could've," Buck said. Buck reached over and picked up the dodger. "How about answering a question for me, before you die?"

"Might as well," the bounty hunter replied. "Ain't got no secrets left in this world."

"How'd you come by this dodger?"

"Hell, Mister, they're all over the territory," the bounty hunter said. "You're goin' to have people doggin' you night and day 'til you wind up just like me, flat on your back, with a bullet in your gizzard."

"Who put them out?" Buck asked. "I'm not wanted for any crime."

"Why, the new marshal of Barlow put them out."

"Who is the new marshal?"

"The one they call Ruthless," the bounty hunter said. He tried another laugh which, again, deteriorated into a spasmatic fit of coughing. "Ain't that a laugh, though?" The bounty hunter stiffened, then died with one last death rattle.

CHAPTER 10

IT WAS MIDAFTERNOON OF THE NEXT DAY, and the sun was a brilliant orb, halfway down its western transit, when Buck saw the town of New Commerce rising into view on the plains before him. Sunlight shimmered off the shingled roofs and clapboard sidings of the dozen or so buildings of the town. The tallest structure of the town was the water tower, down by the depot.

It was this water tower which had drawn Buck to New Commerce. Actually, it wasn't the tower, but what the tower symbolized, for New Commerce was on the railroad line that served Barlow.

The town of New Commerce was living up to its name. Board sidewalks clattered with the footsteps of men and women who were tending to their daily business, a couple of full freight wagons lumbered down the single dirt street, while, over at the leathergoods store, rendering pots simmered and stunk, as hides were being tanned.

Buck rode right through the town to the railroad station, then he opened the door and stepped inside. The station master and the telegrapher were engaged in an intense conversation about Lily Langtry. The question seemed to be whether or not she was more beautiful that Cleopatra. The trainmaster was sure that she was.

"Don't get me wrong," the telegrapher said. "I ain't sayin' she ain't prettier than Cleopatra. I'm just sayin' that there ain't no one alive who ever seen Cleopatra, so there's no way of knowin'."

"Didn't anyone ever draw a picture of Cleopatra?" the station master wanted to know.

"I don't know. I don't think so."

"Then how the hell do we know if she was even pretty at all, let alone prettier than Lily Langtry? No sir, I'm tellin' you that Lily Langtry is the prettiest woman what ever lived, and I'm stickin' by that claim," the stationmaster said. He turned his attention to Buck. "What can I do for you, Mister?"

"What time is the next train for Barlow?"

"It'll leave at midnight."

"Midnight? You don't have anything any sooner? Not even a freight?"

"A freight leaves at ten," the stationmaster said.

"But it'll be shunted off the track so many times that the train that leaves at midnight will get there faster."

"All right," Buck said. "I want a ticket for myself and I want to put my horse on the stock car."

"I have to say, you don't look like the others," the stationmaster said. "You sure you want to go there?"

"What others?"

"All the others that've been flockin' to Barlow. They're the very dregs of the earth, if you ask me. The word is, Barlow is an open town now. You sure you want to go?"

"Yes," Buck said. "I'm sure."

"That'll be nine dollars," the stationmaster said. "Six for you, three for your horse."

Buck paid for the tickets. "Where's a good place to eat supper?" he asked.

"You might try Lamberts, just down the street there, on the left," the stationmaster said. "Nothin' fancy there, just good, home-style cookin', with, probably, the best rolls you ever tasted."

"Sounds good to me," Buck said. "You'll see that my horse gets on?"

"We'll take care of him," the stationmaster promised.

As Buck walked away from the depot, he was being observed from across the street by a man who stood back in the shadows of the stable, looking out over the top half of the Dutch door. Red Smith studied Buck for a moment, then he turned to Ramsey Jones and Deke Wooley, who were lying, lazily, in a pile of straw in the shade of the interior.

"Hey," Red said. "Hey, you two, wake up. It's him."

"It's who," Deke said. He made no effort to move, or even to open his eyes.

"It's Buck Chaney. I just seen him, plain as day, walkin' from the depot." He smiled broadly. "Didn't I tell you if we'd come here we'd catch him when he come to take the train?"

"You sure it's him?" Deke asked.

"Yeah, I'm sure. I've sat across the card table from him a few times. I know him."

Deke sighed and stood up, then began brushing the straw from his clothes. He kicked Ramsey on the bottom of his boot. "Get up, Ramsey," he said. "We're about to make ourselves five hunnert dollars apiece."

Buck had just picked up a second piece of fried chicken, a drumstick, when he was aware that someone was approaching his table. When he looked up, he knew that he had seen him before, but, for a moment, it didn't come to him where. Then he remembered playing poker with him a few times and, remembering that, the man's name came back to him. The fact that the man was redheaded and had a face full of freckles, helped.

"Hello, Red," Buck said easily. "Haven't seen you in a while."

Red licked his lips and wiped sweat from his forehead. His eyes darted about nervously.

"What's got you so rattled, Red?" Buck asked. The friendly tone had left Buck's voice now, for the man's nervousness had instantly alerted Buck to possible danger.

"I'm a deputy marshal now, Chaney," Red said. He cleared his throat. "I'm a deputy over at Barlow."

"I'm real sorry to hear that, Red," Buck said. "I always knew that you weren't worth much, but I never knew you were so low-down that you would side yourself with a no-count skunk like Ruthless Blanton."

At the sound of Ruthless' name, everyone else in the cafe began to pay closer attention to the conversation between the two men, one standing, and the other sitting at the table, eating.

"There's paper out on you, Chaney. You're worth fifteen hundred dollars, dead or alive."

"Not to the law, I'm not," Buck replied. "Only to Ruthless Blanton."

"Yeah, well, like you say, he's the man I'm working for," Red said. "I'm going to have to take you in, Chaney."

"What if I don't want to be taken in?"

"Then, I reckon I'll have to kill you," Red said. The other diners gasped, but Buck calmly spread some butter on one of the rolls and took a bite.

"Didn't you hear what I said?" Red asked. "I said either you come in with me, or I'll have to kill you."

"I heard you," Buck said, chewing easily. By now, all conversation was stopped and all utensils were laid down as the diners watched with morbid curiosity, the drama being played out before them.

"Then why are you just sittin' there, eatin' like nothin's happenin'?" Red demanded.

"Because I'm hungry," Buck answered. "And if I don't eat now, I won't be able to eat later." He smiled. "Like you say, Red, there's about to be a killing. And every time I have to kill someone, it dulls my appetite."

"What if I kill you?"

"Well, that's all the more reason I should eat now, isn't it?" Buck asked. "You see, I really like fried chicken, and I don't reckon they'll be serving it in hell, tonight."

"No, I reckon not," Red agreed. "Go ahead and eat your fried chicken, Chaney. Then when you're finished, come on outside. I'll be waitin' for you in the street."

Buck waited until the door closed behind Red, then he went back to his meal, aware that everyone else in the restaurant was watching him closely, to see how he would react. Buck smiled at them, then toasted them, silently, with a cup of coffee.

"Look at him," one woman whispered, unaware that she could be heard. "He's sitting there eating as calmly as if he didn't have a worry in the world. I couldn't do that. I'd be scared to death."

Despite the calm exterior, Buck did have a few worries, and he would have been an absolute fool not to have some fear. Any gunfight, regardless of how good Buck might be, and how bad his opponent might be, posed some danger...and a prudent man was aware of that danger.

In this case there was a danger that Buck couldn't quite put his finger on. He knew that Red was no match for him in a gunfight, and, more importantly, he knew that Red knew that as well. The question bothering Buck then, was how Red could stand up there so calmly, and issue an invitation to Buck to meet him in the street outside for a fair gunfight. The answer, Buck realized, was that it wasn't going to be fair. Red had something up his sleeve...Buck just didn't know, yet, what it was.

"Waiter," he called.

"Y-yes sir?" the waiter replied nervously.

"What kind of pie do you have?"

"Apple and cherry," the waiter replied.

"Bring me a piece of apple pie," Buck said. "And melt a piece of cheese on top, will you?"

"Yes, sir," the waiter said, shaking his head in

amazement over a man who could eat so calmly, when sudden death might be awaiting him outside.

A few minutes later, Buck finished the last of his pie, then he wiped his mouth with a table napkin and put it on his empty plate. He looked out at the other diners and saw that they had all stopped eating and were watching him intently. When he pulled his pistol, several of them gasped, and one of the men dived under his table in fear.

"You folks ought to go ahead and eat," Buck said easily. "Your food's getting cold." Nervously, as if his suggestion had been an order, many of the diners began eating. Ignoring them, Buck turned the cylinder on his pistol slowly, checking the loads in each chamber. Then he stood up, slipped the pistol back in his holster, and started for the door.

In a town the size of New Commerce, news of an impending gunfight had spread like wildfire. The single street of the little town, which but a moment before had been occupied with daily commerce, was now emptying itself. Men and women scurried down the sidewalks, their boots and shoes clumping loudly upon the boards as they stepped in, or behind buildings to get out of the line of fire. Even the horses and wagons had been moved off the street as nervous owners feared they might get hit by a stray bullet. Most of the townspeople did, however, find positions of safety which would also afford them a vantage point from which they could see everything that was going on, and several of the diners moved to the front windows and door of the restaurant to see the conclusion of the drama that had started in their midst.

When Buck stepped outside, he saw Red about one hundred feet away, standing alone in the middle of the street. Red was holding his hand over his pistol as Buck moved out to face him.

"Where are the others?" Buck called.

"What…what others?" Red replied.

"I know you, Red," Buck said. "If you thought you had to go up against anyone, alone, you'd puke your guts out."

"You're wrong," Red replied. "I don't need no others to handle the likes of you. This, here, is just between me and you. Now, are you goin' to make a fight out of it, or are you goin' to tuck your tail a'twixt your legs and run like the yellow-bellied coward you are?"

Before Buck could answer Red's taunt, a bullet fried the air just beside his ear, hit the dirt beside him, then skipped off with a high-pitched whine. The sound of the rifle shot reached him at about the same time as the bullet, and as Buck dropped and rolled to his left, his gun was already in his hand. Looking toward the sound of the shot, Buck saw a rifleman standing on the porch roof of the general store, just behind a large sign. He saw the gunman operating the cocking lever on his rifle to jack in another round.

Buck didn't give him time for a second shot. He fired at him and his bullet flew true. The rifle dropped to the ground as the ambusher grabbed his throat, then pitched forward, turning a half-flip in the air to land flat on his back, sending up a little puff of dust from the impact of his falling body.

"Ramsey!" Red shouted in fear. "He got Deke!"

By now Red had his own pistol out and firing, but Buck, with his keen instinct for survival, had rolled back to his right after his first shot. As a result, Red's bullet crashed harmlessly into the wooden front stoop of an establishment known as Laraby's Emporium. From inside the emporium a woman screamed in fear as she realized how close that bullet was to what she had assumed would be a safe vantage point.

From his prone position, Buck fired at Red and hit him in the knee. Red let out a howl and went down. He was still firing and Buck felt a bullet tear through the crown of his hat. By now the one Red had called Ramsey had entered the fight, and he raised up and fired from behind the watering trough in front of the Chinese laundry.

Ignoring Ramsey for the time being, Buck threw another shot toward Red, but Red, taking a page from Buck's own book, rolled to get out of the way, thus making himself a more difficult target.

"Ramsey! Ramsey, can you get him?" Red shouted.

"I'm tryin'!" the man behind the watering trough answered. He raised up and fired again, and this time his bullet came close enough that Buck could hear it as it whined by.

Buck knew that he couldn't stay out in the open, so he got up and ran across the street, bending low and firing as he did so. He dived behind the porch of the barbershop then rose and saw that he had a perfect shot at Ramsey. He fired, saw Ramsey drop his pistol in the watering trough, then fall back with blood oozing out of the bullet hole in his chest.

By now Red had managed to improve his own position, and he fired again at Buck. His bullet sent splinters of wood into Buck's face, and Buck put his hand up then pulled it away, peppered with his own blood.

Buck stared across the street, trying to find an opening for a shot. Then he smiled. Red had improved his position by getting out of the street and behind a wooden bench in front of a dressmaker's shop. What he didn't realize, though, was that the large mirror in the window of the dressmaker's shop showed his reflection, and from across the street, Buck watched as Red inched along on his belly to the far end of the bench. Buck took slow and deliberate aim at the end of the bench where he knew Red's face would appear.

Slowly, Red peered around the corner of the bench to see where Buck was and what was going on. Buck cocked his pistol and waited. When enough of Red's head was exposed to give him a target, Buck squeezed the trigger. The Colt .44 roared and bucked in his hand. A cloud of smoke billowed up then floated away. When the cloud cleared, Buck saw Red lying face down in the dirt with a pool of blood spreading out from under his head.

Buck stood up then and started pushing the empty cartridges out of his pistol, replacing them with fresh loads. He looked around the town for anyone else who might be wanting to try him, but saw only the townspeople, emerging now from their places of safety, moving cautiously out into the street to examine with morbid curiosity the bodies of the three men Buck had just killed.

Buck let out a long, slow breath, then leaned back against the railing as he slipped the pistol back into its scabbard. He looked across the street toward the front of Lambert's Restaurant, and saw several of the diners who had witnessed the beginning of the altercation, now outside to witness its conclusion.

"You're Buck Chaney?" a man with a badge asked, coming across the street toward Buck.

"Yes," Buck replied, instantly alert to the lawman's presence. "Are you going to try and collect on the wanted posters?"

"The wanted posters? Hell no," the lawman scoffed. "As far as I'm concerned, those things aren't even legal. I got a batch of them in yesterday, but I burned them. I won't even let them be posted."

"I'm glad someone, somewhere, has a little sense," Buck said.

"I hear you're taking the midnight train back to Barlow," the marshal said.

"That's right."

"Where you goin' to be 'til then?"

"Thought I'd hang around the saloon," Buck said. "If you've no objections."

"No objections. I just wanted to know because I plan to keep an eye open to make sure someone else doesn't try this."

"Thanks," Buck said.

"Listen, Chaney, I don't know exactly what's goin' on over there in Barlow," the lawman said. "But I do know that Dan Efrem was a friend of mine. If you're plannin' on settlin' accounts with Ruthless Blanton, you got my best wishes. But, be careful, will you?"

"I plan to be, Marshal. I plan to be," Buck said.

CHAPTER 11

THE ONLY CONCESSION THE ANGRY BULL saloon made to decoration was to hang a painting on the wall behind the bar. The painting was of a reclining nude woman, to which an anonymous marksman had, long ago, added his own improvement by shooting three bullet holes in the appropriate places. Unfortunately, one shot was slightly off-center so the poor lady had to suffer the indignity of having two nipples on her right breast.

The main room of the Angry Bull was quite large, larger even than the main room of the Easy Pickin's. There were at least a dozen tables in the main room, as well as two potbelly stoves. It was summer, so the stoves stood cold, though soot, discolored metal, and the faint smell of burned wood, indicated that the stoves had been used.

The place was packed, not with the town's nor-
mal population, but with outsiders who had come
in to take advantage of Ruthless Blanton's offer to
open up the town. Though there were several men
hanging around, and most were drinking, there was
surprisingly little money among them because they
were, for the most part, men who were failures, even
in their chosen profession of villainy. An indication
of the lack of resources among them was the fact
that at one table a card game was in progress for
tobacco and matches. The players were contesting
each hand as vigorously as if a great deal of money
was at stake.

Titus Lattimore was standing at the end of the
bar nearest the door, nursing a warm, flat beer,
when an employee from the telegraph office stepped
inside and looked around.

"Has anyone seen Ruthless Blanton?" the telegraph messenger asked.

"What do you want with him?" Lattimore asked.

"I have a message for him."

"I'm his deputy. I'll take it."

"I can't do that. The message is for Ruthless
Blanton hisself."

"Hey!" Lattimore called. "Has anyone seen Ruthless?"

"He said he was goin' over to his office for a little
while," someone answered.

"His office? Hell, I thought this was his office," someone else said, and the others laughed.

"Give me the message," Lattimore growled. "I'll take it down to him."

"I told you, I can't..." before the messenger was able to finish his sentence, Lattimore reached out and snatched the little yellow envelope from his hand.

"Well, now, you didn't give it to me," Lattimore said. "I took it."

The messenger stood there for a moment, undecided as to what he should do next. Then, with a shrug of his shoulders he turned and left, deciding, realistically, that there was nothing he could do.

Lattimore finished his beer, then left the Angry Bull and walked down toward the marshal's office. When he pushed the door open to the marshal's office, he saw Ruthless sitting behind the marshal's desk, with his pistol spread out in pieces on the desk in front of him. He was running a swab through the barrel. He looked up as Lattimore came in.

"The boys havin' a good time?" he asked.

"I reckon so," Lattimore answered. "Say, Ruthless, you got a message here, from Buck Chaney."

"Buck Chaney sent me a message?"

"Yeah."

"Where did the message come from? We'll send word to Red, Ramsey, and Deke, where they can find him."

"Oh, they found him all right," Lattimore grunted. "Read the message."

"You read it to me," Ruthless said.

Lattimore cleared his throat, then read aloud: "I just killed Red Smith, Ramsey Jones, and Deke Wooley. Now I'm coming after you. I'll be there on the morning train. Meet me at the depot and we can settle this, very quickly. Buck Chaney."

Ruthless was silent for a moment, then he picked up another swab and returned to work on the pistol.

"Buck Chaney seems to be a fairly capable man," he finally said.

"Yeah, I guess he's pretty good, all right," Lattimore said. He smiled. "But you can take him. I got no doubt about that."

Ruthless held the barrel up to the light and sighted through it.

"Oh, I'm sure I could take him in a fair fight," Ruthless said. "But who says I have to fight him fair?"

Lattimore chuckled. "You got a plan?"

"He says he's comin' in on the mornin' train," Ruthless replied. "You'll just have a little welcoming committee for him."

"Yeah," Lattimore said. "Yeah," he added giggling. "That's a good idea. I'll get some of the boys together, and we'll meet him the moment he steps down from the train."

"Barlow," the conductor said, walking through the car to wake the passengers. "Folks, this is Barlow. The train will be here for five minutes." Buck, who had been awakened by the conductor's announcement, sat up in his seat and rubbed his eyes, then ran his hand through his hair. He looked through the window, and though it was still dark, he could make out Candlestick Rock. That gave him his bearings, so he knew they would be coming into town in just a couple more minutes.

Only three people seemed to be getting off in Barlow. The remaining passengers settled down more deeply into their chairs, hoping to be able to sleep on through the stop. Buck got up also, but, whereas the other detraining passengers were preparing to get off at the station, Buck decided he would leave the train right here. He stepped out onto the vestibule, then, waiting until the train slowed even more, he hopped down onto the ground. His timing was such that he only had to trot a few steps to regain his balance. Then he moved off through the dark, turning away from the track, while the train rumbled on into town and to the depot.

The depot platform was well-lighted, not only by the lanterns which burned at the comers of the wooden platform, but also by the lights which shined out from the building itself. There were several people on hand to meet the train, some who would be leaving with it, and some who were meeting arriving passengers. The mail wagon was there for the incoming mail. There were four people there to meet the train who stood away from the others. They were a hard, mean-looking group, and all of them were armed. When they heard the whistle and saw the approaching light of the train, they turned to Titus Lattimore.

"Well, here she comes," Lattimore said, though his declaration wasn't necessary. "Finn, when it stops, you get on the track and stand behind it. Keep your eyes on both sides of the train…make sure no one gets off without bein' seen. Johnson, you get on up front of the train an' do the same. Me and LeRoy will get on board."

Finn and Johnson took their positions, while Lattimore and LeRoy got on the train. Lattimore got on up front, and LeRoy got on in the rear. To Lattimore had fallen the job of looking into each berth, and he went about it with the air of someone who was obviously enjoying his work.

"What's goin' on here? Who the hell are you?" a man shouted, when the curtain to his berth was abruptly pulled open. A woman screamed and a little girl began crying, but it didn't stop Lattimore from jerking each curtain open to allow him to look inside.

"Here, Sir!" the conductor shouted, coming into

the sleeping car. "What are you doing? These are paying passengers!"

"And I'm a deputy marshal," Lattimore said, showing the conductor his badge. "Now, if you don't want me to throw you in jail, you'll step out of the way an' let me go about my business."

"Is your business waking innocent passengers?" one woman asked indignantly.

"My business ain't none of your business, lady, so why don't you keep your mouth shut and get back in bed."

"Well, I never," the woman gasped.

"From the looks of you, ma'am, I'd say you're probably right. You never," Lattimore replied. He laughed loudly at this own joke.

When Lattimore finished the sleeping car, he started into the day coach just behind. Here, passengers were trying to sleep also, though they were slumped or slouched in their seats, much less comfortably than the passengers in the car ahead. Lattimore met LeRoy halfway through the car. "Anything back there?" he asked.

"Nothin'," LeRoy growled. "Well, three people got off. But it was an old man, a woman, and a kid. None of 'em was Chaney, that's for sure."

Lattimore expectorated on the floor of the car, then wiped the back of his hand across his mouth.

"Yeah, well, that's pretty much as I expected.

I 'spects Mr. Chaney was just spoutin' off. I can't really see him comin' after Ruthless. Come on, we'll go back and tell him there wasn't anyone on the train."

Buck was pretty sure there would be a welcoming committee waiting for him at the depot. He had sent Ruthless a telegram, telling him he would be arriving on the train, just to make certain there would be. That way, with everyone concentrating on his arrival at the depot, he would be able to sneak into town, unobserved.

Buck didn't really care much for the idea of sneaking into town like a pup with his tail between his legs, but he didn't have much choice. He was going to have to take a look around to see what was going on before he could do anything. And the best way to do that was if no one knew he was here.

Though it was not yet dawn, Barlow was a town of industrious men and women, so several of its citizens were already awake. There was activity down at the depot. Over at the livery a couple of teamsters were hitching up a team. For many of the women today was wash day and behind half a dozen houses fires had already been started and soap was being rendered for the day's labors. Two of the washerwomen were calling back and forth to each other, their private conversation fair game to anyone who cared to listen in. A cock crowed. A baby cried.

Buck moved up the alleyway behind the main row of buildings. The alley reeked of discarded garbage and outdoor toilets, and once he scared up a cat which hissed, then bounded away, startling him into drawing his gun. Finally he reached the back of the Easy Pickin's Saloon. The Easy Pickin's was one of the few buildings in town which had been painted, and it gleamed a bright white in the early morning moonlight.

There was no outside stairway to the second floor of the Easy Pickin's, but there was a drainpipe. There was also a mansard roof which protruded a couple of feet from the side of the building, just below the second floor windows. Buck had no trouble in climbing the drainpipe, then he moved along the mansard roof until he reached the first window. When he tried it, he found that it wasn't locked, so he lifted it, stepped inside, then put the window back down. He was now in the dark hallway of the second floor of the Easy Pickin's Saloon, and no one even knew that he was in town.

Buck moved softly and silently down the hallway until he reached Lily's room. He knocked quietly. A moment later he felt, more than heard, footsteps moving to the door from inside.

"Sam? Sam, is that you?" Lily's muffled voice called out.

"No! It's me, Buck!" Buck hissed.

There was the rattle of a lock being turned, then the door opened and Lily greeted Buck with open arms.

"Oh, Buck!" she said. "Buck, am I glad to see you!"

"I came as soon as I heard," Buck said. "Don't you worry about a thing, Lily. I'm goin' to put things right around here.'

"And just how do you plan to do that, Little Brother?" Lance suddenly asked from the door that led into Lily's bedroom.

"What the hell?" Buck gasped, jerking away from Lily in surprise. "Lance! You're...you're alive!"

Lance chuckled. "That's what they tell me," he said. "But I'm not sure I would swear to it." "But, I thought—" Buck stammered.

"That's what we want people to think," Lily said. "At least for now. I'm sorry I couldn't tell you, but, I couldn't take a chance on the telegram. Since Ruthless and his deputies have taken over the town, they have their fingers into everything that goes on. I'm sure I couldn't get a telegram out without them reading it."

"Yeah," Buck said. "Yeah, you're probably right. But why this? Why pretend that you're dead?"

"When it first started, I didn't have anything to do with it," Lance said.

"It was Doc's idea to begin with," Lily explained. "He examined Lance after Ruthless shot him and saw that he was alive, but was afraid that Ruthless would shoot him again, so, he told everyone that Lance was dead."

"They've already had my funeral, Little Brother," Lance said. "You should have been here. They tell me it was quite an affair."

"Why are you still carrying it on?" Buck asked. "Well, at first, it was just to get Lance away from the saloon," Lily said. "But then we thought, why not let everyone continue to think that. This way, Lance has a chance to heal before Ruthless comes after him again."

"Ruthless won't be coming after him again," Buck said.

"What makes you say that?"

"Because I'm going after Ruthless, first."

"Buck, no, you can't," Lily said. She turned to Lance. "Lance, you stop him. He's your brother."

"I don't want to stop him," Lance said. "Lance? You can't mean that!" Lily said.

"I do mean it," Lance said. "Buck has come here to kill that sonofabitch, and if there was ever anyone who needed killin', it is Ruthless Blanton."

"But you saw him. You know how fast he is. He beat you and Dan Efrem. What makes you think Buck can beat him?"

"Oh, I don't think Buck can beat him," Lance said.

"What?" Buck said. "Well, thanks a lot for the confidence, Big Brother."

Lance chuckled. "What I mean is, I don't think you can beat him if you try to take him the way Dan and I did. But there is a way to beat him."

"How, by shooting him in the back?" Buck asked. "Because if that's what it takes, then I'll do it. I want the sonofabitch dead."

"We won't have to do that," Lance promised. "What I have in mind will give us as much an edge as if we were going to shoot him in the back. It just won't look as bad," he added with a chuckle.

CHAPTER 12

WHEN THE EASY PICKIN'S REOPENED THE next day it was filled with its regular customers who were eager to get away from the rough crowd which normally frequented the Angry Bull. The black wreath was taken down from the door, the piano player was told to play only the merriest of tunes, and the girls were told to smile and be on their best behavior.

Though neither Ruthless nor Lattimore came during the whole day, they were both in just after sunset. Sam set them each up with a drink, on the house.

"On the house?" Ruthless asked.

"The boss's orders," Sam said, nodding toward Lily, who was standing down at the far end of the bar.

Ruthless picked his glass up and held it toward

her. "I don't know if I should drink this or not," he said. "The last time I was in here, you tried to shoot me. Now I come in and you give me a free drink. What am I supposed to think?"

"You're supposed to think that I'm a smart girl," Lily said, smiling at him as she sidled down the bar toward him. "I know which way the wind blows. Why do you think I was so good to Chaney? It's because he was the law around here. Now, you're the law around here. You and your deputy here."

"Yeah," Lattimore said, chuckling. "Yeah, that's right. We are the law." He started to drink his drink but Ruthless put out his hand to stop him. Ruthless smiled at Lily, but the smile didn't reach his eyes.

"I'm sure there is something to what you say," Ruthless said. "Still, a fella in my position has to be very cautious. How do I know you haven't poisoned these drinks?"

Lattimore, realizing now why Ruthless stopped him from taking a drink, sat his glass down as quickly as if it had burned his hand.

"Sam?" Lily called.

"Yes, Miss Lily?" the bartender replied, coming down to the end of the bar.

"Sam, our motives are being questioned. I want you to drink one of these drinks," Lily said.

"Yes, ma'am," Sam said, easily. He picked up Lattimore's drink and tossed it down. "Will that be all?" he asked.

"Does that convince you?" Lily asked Ruthless.

"It convinces me that you weren't trying to poison Lattimore. But then, it wasn't Lattimore who killed your man, was it?"

"Mr. Blanton, you seen me pour them drinks," Sam said. "They both come out of the same bottle."

"But they are different glasses," Ruthless said. He slid his glass across the bar toward Lily. "I'd be obliged if you would drink from my glass," he invited.

"Be glad to," Lily said easily. She held the glass up. "Cheers," she said, before she tossed it down.

"Well, good. Now that that's settled, I'll have another," Ruthless said.

Lily held up her finger. "Huh, uh. You only get one free one a night. This one, you pay for."

"But you drank the…" Ruthless started, then he chuckled. "All right," he said. "You've made your point. I'll pay for them. If you'll sit with me while I drink it," he added.

"If you want company, I'll get one of the girls," Lily suggested.

"No. I want you. That's your job, isn't it? To keep your customers happy?"

Lily sighed. "All right," she said. She nodded toward a nearby table. "Bring the drinks over there, Sam."

Lily, Ruthless, and Lattimore sat at the table and

Sam came around the bar, carrying the bottle and two glasses.

"Say, bartender," Ruthless said, as Sam picked up the coin and began pouring the drinks. "I thought you told me I had to worry about Chaney's brother."

"That's what I said," Sam replied.

"Well, it turns out he's nothing but blow. He sent me a telegram telling me he would be on the train this morning, but he never showed up."

"Maybe he got detained," Sam said.

"Maybe he got scared," Lattimore suggested with a laugh.

Suddenly there was a loud, high-pitched scream from the top floor. It was a blood-curdling sound which brought an instant halt to all conversation in the place. Even the piano stopped as everyone looked up toward the second floor landing. One of the bar girls had run to the rail and she was looking over, onto the floor below. Her hair was frazzled and there was a wild look in her face.

"Jenny!" Lily shouted. "Jenny, what is it?"

"It's him, Miss Lily! I saw him, plain as day!" Jenny called down. She pointed down the hall behind her.

"Who? You saw who, plain as day?"

"Why, Lance Chaney," Jenny said. "He was...he was—" Jenny fainted before she could complete what she was trying to say.

"Lance Chaney? What's she talkin' about?" someone asked as an excited buzz of conversation broke out among the customers.

Lily and half a dozen others dashed up the stairs. By the time they got there, Jenny was coming to.

"Oh!" she said, when she saw Lily. "Oh, Miss Lily, it was awful."

"There, there, it's all right, now," Lily said. "Now you just tell us what you saw...or what you think you saw."

"I did see it, Miss Lily. I wasn't just seein' things. It was there."

"It?" Ruthless asked. Lily noticed that his voice was a little more high-pitched and excited than usual.

"The ghost."

"Nonsense, there's no such thing as a ghost."

"Well, I don't know what else it could've been," Jenny said. "But when I looked down toward Mr. Chaney's room a moment ago, I saw someone standing just outside the door. Well, I remember how you said that no one was to go in that room, Miss Lily, so I started toward him. 'You can't go in there, that door's locked,' I told him. Then he, or it, or whatever it was, turned to me and smiled, and that was when I seen that it was Lance Chaney."

"Lance Chaney?"

"But he's dead."

"Impossible."

"Hush," Lily said to the customers who had all begun to talk at the same time. "Let her tell her story. Go on, Jenny. This...thing you think you saw. Did it say anything?"

"Yes'm. He said, 'Oh, Jenny, locked doors don't bother me, anymore.' And with that he just sort of...sort of..."

"What?"

"Well, he just sort of went right through the door," Jenny said. "Like it wasn't even there." The others gasped.

"There can't nothin' do that."

"Nothin' human."

"Do you reckon she really did see a ghost?"

"Shut up! All of you!" Ruthless shouted. "That's the most ridiculous thing I've ever heard. Save your ghost stories for the children."

"Yeah," Lattimore said. "Anyway, even if he could come back, why would he be wantin' to come here?"

"Well, you know the answer to that, don't you, Mr. Blanton?" Sam asked.

"Me? No, why should I know why he would want to come back?"

"Perhaps you have forgotten. But, just before you shot him Lance said, 'If I have to, I'll come back from hell.' I reckon that's what he's doin'. He's come back for you, Mr. Blanton."

Ruthless jerked, then took two quick steps backward. His eyes darted around like the eyes of some trapped rodent. "What…what are you trying to do?" Ruthless asked. "Stop it, all of you. You," he said, pointing to Lily. "Open that door."

"I'm not sure that I can," Lily replied.

"What do you mean, you're not sure you can? You own the place, don't you?"

"Yes, but Lance had the only key to the room. He locked it when he left and it's still locked."

"Are you telling me you didn't take the key from him before you buried him?"

"You'll have to take that up with the undertaker, Mr. Albritton," Lily said. "I didn't, personally, go through his clothes. I was a little bit too upset, if you recall."

"Lattimore, go over to the undertaker's parlor and get Albritton over here," Ruthless ordered. "What if he is busy?"

"Busy? I don't care if the sonofabitch is up to his ass in corpses. I want him over here."

"All right, Ruthless, sure, I'll get him. Anything you say."

"Suppose the rest of us go on back downstairs now?" Lily suggested to the others who had been drawn to the scene by their curiosity.

"No," Ruthless said quickly.

"No? No, what?"

"The rest of us ain't goin' back downstairs. They

can go," he said, pointing to all the customers. "But you stay. And the girl, here, stays. And the bartender."

"But, whatever for?" Lily asked, confused by Ruthless' curious order.

"There is somethin' goin' on here," Ruthless said. "There is somethin' goin' on and I aim to find out what it is."

"Please, Miss Lily, don't make me stay here," Jenny said. "I can't stay here, I'm too frightened. It was him, I tell you. I saw him."

"And you seen him just go right through the door," Ruthless scoffed.

"Yes."

"You, more than anyone, are going to stay here," Ruthless said. "You're the one that started all this. I'm going to show you once and for all that there's nothing in that room."

"You're right," Jenny said. "I didn't see nothin'. I just made it all up. I was funnin', that's all. See?" Jenny forced a hysterical laugh. "It was just a big joke."

"No," Ruthless said. "Now you are lyin'. You did see somethin' didn't you?"

"No," Jenny said quietly.

"You did. And I aim to find out what it was. Soon as Lattimore gets here with the undertaker and the key, we're goin' in there."

"No, please!" Jenny pleaded. "Don't make me go in there!"

"Where is that fool undertaker, anyway?" Ruthless asked in exasperation.

"Hold your horses, hold your horses, I'm comin'," Albritton said, coming up the stairs at that moment. "I'm not used to hurryin' to get anywhere. You are a little different from most of my customers. They generally have the virtue of patience." He laughed at his own joke.

"I'm not one of your customers," Ruthless said. "And from the looks of things, I don't intend to be. According to the girl here, one of your customers is still walkin' around."

Albritton chuckled. "You mean a ghost? No such thing."

"Are you sure about that?" Ruthless asked. "Mister, if I thought there was such a thing as ghosts, do you think I could do this job?"

"So what you're saying is, this girl didn't see a ghost," Ruthless declared.

"She may have seen something, but she didn't see a ghost."

"Well, now we're goin' to prove it. The lady here says that Chaney had the only key to this room."

"That's right," Albritton said. "He had a key in his pocket."

"I don't suppose you buried it with him, did you?"

"No, of course not. That would be a foolish thing to do." Albritton took the key from his pocket.

"Here it is, Miss Lily. I'm sorry I haven't gotten around to giving it to you yet."

"That's all right," Lily replied. "I don't think I could have faced looking at all his things before now, anyway."

"Open the door," Ruthless ordered.

Albritton fiddled with the lock, then the door swung open. It was dark in the room, and a strong smell issued from inside.

"What is that smell?" Lattimore asked, waving his hand in front of his nose.

Albritton sniffed. "Why, it's embalming fluid," he said.

"God, it's awful," Ruthless complained. "What did you do, spill it all over you?"

"No, I haven't been around any embalming fluid since the day I buried..." Albritton paused in mid-sentence.

"Since the day you buried who?" Lattimore asked.

"Lance Chaney," Albritton said in a small voice.

"My God, that proves it!" Jenny said. "He was here! You can still smell the embalming fluid."

"That doesn't prove anything," Ruthless said. "Except, maybe, that you are all crazy."

"I'll light a lamp," Lily said. She opened the top drawer of a chest and pulled out a lucifer, struck it, and held it to the wick of the kerosene lantern.

A moment later when she had the flame adjusted, the room was filled with a bubble of golden light. "Now," she said. "We can have a good look around."

Ruthless stood there, looking around the room in fear and confusion. His eyes caught a glint of the lantern and with the demonic expression on his face and the cold glint in his pupils, it didn't stretch things too far to imagine he was standing in the portals of hell.

"There!" Ruthless said after a moment's examination. "There, do you see? There's nothin' in here. You were just seein' things, that's…"

"Oh, my God!" Albritton suddenly gasped. He put one hand to his chest and the other to the door frame as if to hold himself up.

"Mr. Albritton! Mr. Albritton, what is it?" Lily asked. "What's wrong?"

"Those things there, on the bed!" Albritton said, pointing to the bed with a bony finger. There, on the bed, were a black suit coat and a tie.

"My God! You're right!" Lily gasped.

"Right about what?" Ruthless demanded. "What are you talking about?"

"Those are the very clothes he was wearing when I buried him," Albritton said.

CHAPTER 13

WORD THAT JENNY HAD SEEN LANCE CHANEY spread all through the town. Within an hour other reported "sightings" began to come in. One man swore he saw Lance standing in the window of his room looking down onto the street below. Another had him riding a horse, and a third swore that he was walking around town, checking the locks on the buildings just as he used to do when he was a deputy, making the night rounds.

"It was just after he come away from checkin' the lock at Ledbetter's, it was," the man telling the story said. "I said, 'Hello, Deputy,' right to his face I did."

"And did he answer you?"

"He sure did. He said, 'Nice night for roamin' around, ain't it, Dixon?' He said it just like that. I mean, for all his bein' a ghost, he knew who I was and he called me by name."

"Well, I ain't goin' to believe it 'til I see him with

my own eyes," one of the others replied.

Ruthless scoffed at all the reports but it was obvious that they were beginning to get to him, because he was drinking a little heavier than usual.

"I think it's working," Lily told Lance and Buck when she went back up to her room. "Right now he's got the shakes so bad that he can barely hold a liquor glass. You were right, Lance, he is frightened of ghosts. How did you know?"

"It was something I noticed, just before he shot me," Lance replied.

"You mean when you told him you'd come back from hell if you had to?"

"Yes. It was just an expression, but it was obvious that he was bothered by it." Lance chuckled. "He wasn't bothered enough for it to do any good then, but it might be paying off now."

"What do you say we get this over with? I think now would probably be a good time to go downstairs and face him," Buck said. He stood up and loosened his gun in his holster.

"No, not yet," Lance said. He smiled. "The longer this goes, the worse he's going to get. Why not enjoy it for a while?"

Lily laughed. "Lance is right, Buck. This is driving Rufus Blanton crazy. You should've seen him when Albritton said that he had buried Lance in the jacket and tie that was on the bed. He turned white as a sheet."

"Mr. Albritton did a good job for us," Lance said. "So did Sam and Jenny. Especially Jenny. I tell you the truth, her scream made chills run down my spine, and I was the ghost," Lance said, laughing.

"Oh, Jenny was thrilled," Lily said, "not only to find out you weren't dead, but also to be able to help. And she said we could count on her if we needed anything else done."

"What else could we do?" Buck asked.

"Something that will keep him on edge," Lily suggested. "But I don't know exactly what."

"What if I make an appearance," Lance suggested.

"No," Lily replied, quickly. "It's much too dangerous. If he sees you, he's liable to shoot you."

"Not if we play our cards right," Lance said. "There's a trapdoor in the floor of the pantry that leads down to the root cellar, right?"

"Yes."

"Suppose I made an appearance at the kitchen door…just long enough for Ruthless to see me. By the time he came over to investigate, I could be into the pantry and down the trapdoor into the root cellar."

"What if he shot first, and investigated later?" Lily asked.

"Well, that's just a chance we'll have to take," Lance said.

"Maybe not," Buck put in. "I might be able to

come up with a small refinement to the plan that would prevent that."

"What kind of refinement?" Lance asked.

"Can we trust the piano player to keep our secret?"

"Of course we can," Lily said.

"Then let's get him in on it," Buck suggested. "We need his help."

Half an hour later Lily was back downstairs, where everyone was still buzzing about the "ghost" of Lance Chaney. Ruthless was sitting alone, at a table near the back wall. That wouldn't do. Lily would have to get him back up to the end of the bar, for it was only from there that he would have the proper angle to see the 'ghost' when it made another appearance.

"Mr. Blanton?" Lily called, smiling broadly at him and holding up a bottle. "Would you care to join me for a drink?"

Ruthless kicked out a chair from the table and gestured toward it. "Why don't you come over here?" he replied.

"I can't do that," she answered. "I need to stay up here to keep an eye on things. Never mind, I'll drink alone. I just thought it might be more enjoyable if I had some company."

Ruthless nodded, then got up from his table and walked over to the bar to join her.

"Where is Mr. Lattimore?" Lily asked.

"He's out checking on things for me," Ruthless answered.

Lily laughed, a low, throaty laugh. "Now, he wouldn't be trying to chase down that ghost for you, would he, Mr. Blanton?" she teased.

"No!" Ruthless said quickly. "I mean, that's ridiculous. There's no such thing as a ghost. The girl was just seeing things, that's all."

"Oh, I quite agree," Lily said. "Jenny always was an impressionable young woman. And Mr. Albritton has buried so many people that there's no way he can remember from corpse to corpse, who was wearing what."

"Can't we find something else to talk about? The whole town is gabbing about this 'ghost' nonsense, and I'm getting sick and tired of it."

"Of course we can," Lily said. "Anyway, why are you worried? I mean, how many men have you killed, anyway? Have any of their ghosts ever come back to haunt you?"

"I said, let's change the subject!" Ruthless said, slamming his glass down on the bar.

"I'm sorry," Lily said sweetly. "I didn't mean anything by it. I was just trying to make pleasant conversation. That's all."

"You have a strange idea of what you call pleasant conversation," Ruthless said.

"Miss Lily?" the piano player asked, coming up

to them at that moment.

"Yes, James, what can I do for you?"

"I was wondering if you would mind if I move the piano?"

"Move the piano?"

"Yes, ma'am," James answered. "If you will recall, I used to have it over there, by the kitchen door, then I moved it back to where it is now. But I think I like it better by the kitchen door. The acoustics are better there."

"Sure, put it wherever you want. You're the one who plays it," Lily said easily.

"Thank you," James said, returning to his piano.

"What does he care where the damn piano is?" Ruthless asked. "No one listens to it."

"Oh, but you're wrong, Mr. Blanton. Why, James' piano playing is one of the things that sets Easy Pickin's apart from the Angry Bull, or any other saloon in the area. Folks come from all around to listen to him. He is an excellent musician."

"Oh, Miss Lily, would you come over here for a moment, please?" Sam called from the other end of the bar.

"I'll be right there," Lily replied. She put her hand on Ruthless' wrist. "Do you see now why I have to stay up here?" she asked. "There is always something for me to attend to. Now, don't you go away. I'll be right back. In the meantime, have another drink on me." Lily refilled Ruthless' glass.

Sam didn't actually need Lily and James didn't really want to move his piano. That was all part of the plan and now, as a couple of men picked up the piano and began moving it under James' guidance, the plan was put into operation. Ruthless was left alone at the end of the bar.

Ruthless took a swallow of his drink, then put the glass down. When he looked up he saw some-one, or something, standing in the kitchen door. The man's face was, literally, as white as chalk, but that didn't keep Ruthless from recognizing him. It was Lance Chaney!

"What the hell?" Ruthless yelled, just as the piano passed between him and Lance. "Stop!"

The two men moving the piano stopped instant-ly, putting the piano down.

"What's wrong, Mr. Blanton?" James asked.

Ruthless pulled his pistol and started toward the door, waving at the men to get the piano out of the way.

"Move it!" he said. "Move that piano, you fools!"

"Do you want it back where it was, Mr. Blanton?" James asked innocently.

"I don't care where you put it, you idiot! Just move it the hell out of my way!"

"Out of your way?" James asked.

"Yes! Out of my way. He was there, you idiot!

Didn't you see him? He was there!"

By now everyone in the saloon was watching the bizarre behavior of Ruthless Blanton and wondering what was going on.

"Mr. Blanton, are you all right?" Lily asked solicitously.

"It was him!" Ruthless said, pointing toward the kitchen door. He couldn't get to the kitchen door, however, because the piano was still there. He pointed his pistol toward the two men who had been moving the piano. "Move the damned piano or I'll kill you where you stand!" he shouted. Quickly, they picked the piano up and moved it back to where it was in the first place.

"It was who?" Lily asked.

"Who? It was Lance Chaney!"

"You saw Lance in the piano?" Lily asked patronizingly.

"No, I didn't see him in the piano!" Ruthless bellowed in exasperation. "He was there, standing in the doorway. Do you mean to tell me you didn't see him? He was right there!"

"But, there was no one there, Mr., Blanton," Lily insisted. "I've been standing right here, all along. Sam, did you see anyone?"

"No, Miss Lily, I didn't see a soul," Sam replied.

"But you had to see him! How could you not have seen him? You were closer to him than I was."

"Well, yes I was, and I had a very good view of

the doorway. It must have been a shadow, or a trick of light," Lily said.

"It wasn't a shadow or a trick of light. It was him, I tell you. It was him. And his face was white, as white as flour."

"Oh, dear, you are convinced that you saw something, aren't you? Would you like to look in the kitchen?"

"Yes," Ruthless said. "Yes, I would."

Lily started toward the kitchen with Sam and Ruthless. Several of the patrons started there as well, but Lily turned toward them.

"Listen, there's no need for all of us to crowd into the kitchen, making a mess of things," she said. "The rest of you just stay out here. As soon as we get Mr. Blanton calmed down, we'll be back."

"What do you mean, get me calmed down?" Ruthless bellowed angrily. "I don't need you to get me calmed down! All I need to do is to find that sonofabitch so I can kill him."

"Which sonofabitch?" Lily asked, sweetly.

"Chaney. Lance Chaney," Ruthless shouted. "Who the hell do you think I'm talking about?"

"Well, I'm not sure, Mr. Blanton," Lily said. "You see, I was under the impression that you had already killed Lance Chaney."

Ruthless glared at Lily for a moment, then charged into the kitchen and began looking around.

"He's in here!" Ruthless said. "Help me find him!"

"There's no one in here, Mr. Blanton."

"He must've gone out back."

"Look at the door," Lily said, calmly. "As you can see, the bolt is set from inside. If he was here and he went out, how could he have reset the bolt?"

"He's somewhere!" Ruthless said. "He couldn't have just disappeared into thin air!"

"Well, I suppose he could if he were a ghost," Lily said.

"What's in there?" Ruthless asked, disregarding Lily's comment, and pointing to another door.

"Just the pantry," Lily replied. "Would you like to search in there, as well?"

"You're damn right I would," Ruthless answered, pushing past her to go into the pantry.

The pantry was a narrow room, lined with shelves. There was no way anyone could be hiding in here. He didn't see what Lily saw…a fine dusting of flour on the floor. Lance must've come up with the idea of flour on the face at the last moment. Lily smiled. She thought it made a nice addition to the plan.

"Mr. Blanton, are you satisfied now that there was no one here?" Lily asked.

With a growl of frustrated rage, Ruthless holstered his pistol, then walked back out into the saloon. The saloon patrons were still quiet, watching with intense interest this latest chapter in the drama of the ghost of Lance Chaney.

"Perhaps another drink would ease your fears," Lily suggested.

"Ease my fears?" Ruthless shouted. "Just who the hell do you think you're talkin' to? I'm Rufus Blanton. Ruthless, they call me, and ruthless I am. Why, I've killed more men than I can count. I'm not afraid of any man alive."

"Alive," Lily repeated.

"Listen, you!" Ruthless shouted, pointing his pistol at her. "All of you!" he added, swinging the gun around toward the entire saloon. Instinctively, men ducked or moved to get out of the way. "To hell with you! To hell with all of you!" Ruthless put his pistol back into his holster, then with one final glare at everyone present, left the saloon, pushing through the bat wings doors so fiercely that they swung back and forth for a few swings before settling down.

"The show's over, folks," Lily said. "James, play a little music."

"Yes, ma'am," James replied, and though he kept the laugh off his face, he couldn't keep it out of his eyes as he and Lily exchanged glances.

CHAPTER 14

SOMEHOW, WORD OF WHAT HAD HAPPENED down in the Easy Pickin's Saloon managed to reach the Angry Bull, ahead of Ruthless. The only way it could have was if someone had been standing right by the door and ran down to the Angry Bull to tell the story as soon as Ruthless encountered his "ghost." However the story got there, it was there, so that by the time Ruthless came into the Angry Bull, people were already talking about it.

"Did you really see Chaney's ghost, Ruthless?" Lattimore asked.

"I don't know," Ruthless said, pouring himself a drink as soon as he sat down. "No, I'm sure I didn't. I mean, there's no such thing as a ghost."

"I didn't think so," Lattimore said. He waved his hand around the room. "But of course, ever'one aroun' here is tellin' the story that you did."

"I saw somethin'," Ruthless said.

"What?"

"Damnit all to hell, I don't know what," Ruthless said. "But there's somethin' funny goin' on aroun' here, and I'd give a lot to find out what."

"How much is a lot?" Lattimore asked. Ruthless had just poured himself another drink when Lattimore asked the question, and now he fixed Lattimore with an intense gaze.

"What do you mean?" he asked.

Lattimore cleared his throat. "You said you would give a lot to find out what's going on. Would you give a hundred dollars?"

"That's a lot of money," Ruthless said.

"You got more'n that left over from that last stage job you did. And that wouldn't be too much to pay for a little peace of mind, would it?" Lattimore asked.

Ruthless tossed the drink down before he answered, then he stroked his chin and studied Lattimore for a long moment.

"I reckon I'd pay that," he finally agreed. "If there's somethin' goin' on around here that I need to know about, and if you think you really can get to the bottom of this 'ghost' business, then it would be worth a hundred dollars."

Lattimore smiled broadly, then poured himself another drink. "Well, I got me an idea that will figure this thing out, once and for all," he said. "You might not like it. I mean, seein' as you have so much respect for the dead, an' all. But it's the only way."

"What do you plan to do?"

"I plan to go down to the graveyard and dig up Lance Chaney's bones." Lattimore laughed. "I figure if we got his body right there where we can see it, it ain't goin' to be wanderin' aroun' searin' folks."

George Toomey heard Lattimore tell Ruthless that he was going down to the graveyard to dig up Lance Chaney. As the town drunk who subsisted for the most part on discarded food and leftover drinks, Toomey had become so much an institution that he tended to blend into the background, like a horse, or a wagon, or a piece of furniture. People could look right at him and not see him, which was why, when he was draining the last swallow of whiskey from glasses left on a table adjacent to the table that was being used by Ruthless and Lattimore, neither one of them even noticed him.

The fact that the town didn't notice Toomey didn't mean that Toomey didn't notice the town. He was very aware of what was going on, everywhere. In fact, because of his unique perspective he was, perhaps, the most aware person in Barlow. Toomey knew that Deputy Chaney wasn't dead, and had known it from the first night. He had been asleep under the porch of the Easy Pickin's when they brought Lance back from Doc Presnell's office, to hide him in Lily's room. And though he hadn't been told, specifically, that the "ghostly appearances" were being perpetrated to unnerve Ruthless Blanton, he figured that out for himself. Toomey knew then, that if Lattimore dug up Lance Chaney's coffin and discovered that the deputy wasn't in the coffin, whatever scheme Lance and the others were trying to pull on Ruthless, would backfire.

Toomey wanted the scheme to work. He had never been a horse, or a wagon, or a piece of furniture to Deputy Chaney. He had been a human being and Chaney had never failed to speak to him, or offer him a coin, or a place to sleep, or a meal. Lily, also, had always treated Toomey like a human being, so if there was any way he could help both of them, he intended to do it.

When Toomey stepped into the Easy Pickin's a few minutes later, he moved unnoticed up to the end of the bar, standing, ironically, exactly where Ruthless had been earlier, when he had "seen the ghost." Lily saw him and, without being asked, she poured him a real drink from a real bottle and set the glass before him.

"Thank you," Toomey said.

"You missed the excitement, Mr. Toomey," Lily said.

"You mean when Ruthless saw Deputy Chaney

and thought he was seeing Banquo's ghost?"

"Banquo's ghost?" Lily replied, amused by the analogy. "Yes, I suppose he might have thought that. She laughed. "You should have seen him. He turned white as a ghost himself."

"Miss Lily, I have some information that you must convey to Deputy Chaney at once."

"What?" Lily asked, surprised by Toomey's remark. "What do you mean, you have information for Deputy Chaney?"

Toomey looked around to make certain he couldn't be overheard, then made a motion for Lily to come closer to him.

"I am privy to the information that Deputy Chaney isn't dead," he said. "I also know that you are keeping him in your room."

"How...how do you know that?" Lily gasped.

"I see things, hear things," Toomey said. "But that isn't important. Your secret is safe with me. What is important is that, a few moments ago, I overheard Ruthless and Lattimore talking. It would seem that Lattimore plans to go down to the graveyard in an attempt to exhume Deputy Chaney's body. If he does that and discovers that there is no body, there could be trouble."

"You're right," Lily said. "There could be big trouble." She drummed her fingers on the bar for a moment, then looked at Toomey and smiled. "Thanks," she said. "Thanks a lot." She slid a half-full bottle of whiskey across the bar toward him, but he slid it back.

"No, ma'am," he said. "It would be better if you didn't give that to me."

"What? Why?"

"Miss Lily, I can't remember the last time I actually had a real bottle of whiskey," Toomey said. "If someone were to see me with a bottle now, they might wonder how I came by it. A really suspicious person might also remember that I was down at the Angry Bull earlier tonight, and they might realize that I overheard Ruthless and Lattimore talking. If this person of a suspicious nature were to put all that together, they would have to conclude that I came by the whiskey by selling you information. And, if they were of a malevolent nature, they might also share that conclusion with Ruthless and Lattimore."

Lily looked at Toomey in complete surprise. That was the longest statement she had ever heard him make and she suddenly realized that he was, or at least at one time had been, a most articulate man. She wondered about him, and about the mystery of his background. How had such a man become a drunken derelict? Whatever might be Toomey's story, he had kept it to himself and she would allow him that privacy for as long as he wished.

"I owe you, Mr. Toomey," she said, quietly.

"No, ma'am," Toomey replied. "You and Deputy Chaney are two of the finest people I've ever run across. It would be my pleasure if this little piece of information proves to be helpful."

It was nearly midnight when Titus Lattimore walked into the graveyard, a shovel in one hand and a bottle of whiskey in the other. He picked his way through the silent, white crosses and boards until he came to the newest grave in the cemetery. The whitewashed grave marker gleamed softly, and the carving was still fresh enough and deep enough to be read, even in the moonlight.

Here lies LANCE CHANEY
Murdered by Ruthless Blanton

"Well, Mr. Murdered Deputy Marshal Lance Chaney," Lattimore said, pausing beside the grave and pulling the cork on the whiskey bottle. "You think you're sleepin' peacefully in there, do you? Well, you've got another think comin'." Lattimore took a long, Adam's apple-bobbing drink from the whiskey bottle, then corked it and set it down beside him. He picked up the shovel and began digging.

For several minutes there was no sound whatever, except for the chunk of the shovel digging dirt, then the heavy breathing, brought on by Lattimore's labor. A cloud passed over the moon and the cemetery grew darker. Out on the prairie a coyote howled and, involuntarily, Lattimore shivered.

"What the hell?" he grunted. "That ain't nothin' but a coyote and I've heard a passel of them in my day." Lattimore reached for the bottle, pulled the cork, took another long drink, recorked the bottle, and returned to digging what had now become quite a sizeable hole.

An owl hooted.

"Latti..."

"More." The sound came from two different places and the name was drawn out, almost in a howl.

"What?" Lattimore replied. He stopped digging and looked around the cemetery. "Who is it? Who's calling me?"

"Latti..."

"More."

Again, the sound came from two different places in the cemetery, starting on one side and ending on the other.

"Who is that?"

"I'm coming..."

"For you…"

"Latti…"

"More."

Lattimore climbed up out of the hole, dropped

his shovel and pulled his gun. "Who's there?" he shouted, looking around anxiously. "Who's calling me?"

"Lance…"

"Chaney."

"Where are you?" Lattimore shouted.

"Over…"

"Here…"

"Latti…"

"More."

Lattimore started firing wildly, shooting to his left and to his right in the direction of the sound. As he fired he turned to run, but that was a mistake because the muzzle flash of his shooting blinded him and he tripped over the shovel and fell, headfirst, down into the hole he had just opened. When he did so it had the same effect as a drop through the trap door on a hangman's gallows. Lattimore's neck was broken and he died, instantly.

Lance Chaney had been on one side of the cemetery and Buck had been on the other. They had worked out the idea of alternating the words as they called out to Lattimore, reasoning that it would make the sound appear to come from everywhere, and nowhere. They figured such a ruse would frighten Lattimore out of the cemetery before he could discover that Lance wasn't really buried there. It worked much better than they thought.

"Damn," Buck said in a stage whisper. He had jumped down into the hole to check on Lattimore. "The sonofabitch is dead."

"I guess it just saves the state the cost of a trial," Lance replied.

"What do you want to do with him?"

"Leave him there," Lance said. "Just like he is."

Buck stood up, then climbed out of the hole. "Yeah," he chuckled. "That should cause a little talk."

The two brothers could hear voices coming from the town.

"Did you hear that shootin'? Where'd it come from?"

"It come from the cemetery. Come on. Let's get out there an' see what's goin' on."

"Buck! Someone's coming," Lance hissed.

"We'll go out the back side," Buck said.

The largest grave marker in the cemetery was that of a man named Colonel Sam Armstrong. Armstrong's grave was at the very rear of the cemetery and it provided enough concealment to allow Lance and Buck to exit the grounds without being seen by any of the curious citizens who were now flocking out to the graveyard from town.

"Look at that!" someone said, pointing to a body that lay sprawled out in the moonlight.

"It's Lattimore."

"What's he doin' here?"

"It's obvious, ain't it? There's the shovel. He was tryin' to dig up Deputy Chaney's body."

"Why"

"I know why," someone else said. "I was down at the Angry Bull when I heard him and Ruthless talkin'. Ruthless allowed as how he would give Lattimore a hundred dollars to dig Chaney up and stop all this talk about him bein' a ghost."

"Yeah, well, he didn't dig him up, but he sure proved he wasn't no ghost."

"How?"

"Hell, you heard all the shootin', didn't you? Since when does a ghost need a gun?"

"I don't reckon a ghost ever needed a gun," someone said. He had jumped down into the hole to examine Lattimore's body. "And I don't reckon Chaney's ghost needed one either. All the shootin' come from Lattimore's gun. Lattimore's body ain't got a mark on it."

There was dead silence for a moment, then someone asked in a quiet, shaky, voice.

"What did you say?"

"I said Lattimore ain't been shot. Ain't been stabbed neither. Far as I can tell, there ain't nothin' happened to him."

"What do you mean there ain't nothin' happened to him? He's dead, ain't he?"

"Oh, yes," the man down in the hole said. "I felt

for his heart an' it ain't beatin'. He's dead, all right. He's dead as a doornail. The question is, how did he die?"

"Why don't we take him into town?" someone suggested. "We can take him to Doc Presnell's office and let the doc take a look at him. I'll bet he could tell us how he died."

The man who had jumped down into the hole with Lattimore now brushed his hands together as if absolving himself of all responsibility and climbed out of the hole.

"You want him in town, you take him into town," he said. "I don't want nothin' to do with it."

"Me neither," another said, and there was a movement toward town, general at first, then somewhat faster, and faster still until, by the time the curious citizens had reached the edge of the cemetery, they were running.

When the men who had gone out to investigate the shooting in the cemetery started running back to town, they encountered a few more citizens whose own curiosity had brought them halfway out to the cemetery.

"What is it?" one of them called. "What are you runnin' for?" His question wasn't answered, but, seeing the others flee from the cemetery was all the incentive the new arrivals needed to turn and run with them. Consequently, Lattimore's body was abandoned by people whose fear was greater, even, than their morbid curiosity.

By the time the little group got back to town the story of a shootout between Lattimore and Lance Chaney's ghost was full-blown and embellished with each telling.

"I seen it all, I tell you," one over-enthusiastic witness reported to the others in the Easy Pickin's Saloon. "There was Lattimore on one side, yellin' and cursin' and blazin' away. And, no more'n fifteen or twenty feet away from him stood Lance Chaney, just as cold as ice and dead as stone. Them bullets just popped right on through Chaney, like he wasn't even there."

"That's 'cause he wasn't there," someone reminded the storyteller.

"Well, maybe he wasn't there hisself," the storyteller replied. "But his ghost sure as hell was."

There was an equal amount of embellishment given the stories being told at the Angry Bull. Ruthless Blanton sat at what had come to be regarded as "his" table, all alone, drinking quietly as he fought against the fear that had become so real that he could taste the bile in his throat.

CHAPTER 15

THERE WERE MANY WHO COULD NOT understand how someone who killed as easily and as readily as Rufus Blanton could be so frightened of death. But that was because they saw and knew him only as "Ruthless" Blanton, a gunfighter whose fast hands and quicker trigger finger had made him the scourge of the West. They saw him from the outside. The fears and terrors which nagged at Ruthless Blanton, however, came from inside, from the deepest recesses of his soul and the darkest corridors of his mind.

It had happened three years ago in a little town which, even though it was on the American side of the border, was so dominated by its Spanish heritage that it could have been in Mexico. Ruthless was eating his lunch in a cantina when he overheard some men talking about the chalice of pure gold that was the pride of the local church. The discussion was whether its weight in gold was worth more than its value as a work of art.

"It was not fashioned by a well-known artisan," one side of the argument ran. "It was fashioned by Padre Sanchez from gold coins and pieces of jewelry donated over the years by the faithful of the church. Surely you can see that the value of the gold is worth more than the value of the art."

"But Padre Sanchez is a gifted artisan," the other side contended.

"And it is a cup made for the faithful, from gifts of the faithful. That makes it more valuable in God's sight, does it not?"

"God does not work in a bank, Señor. I am talking about U.S. dollars. In a bank, a teller will see the chalice only for the gold it contains."

Though not a part of the argument except as an eavesdropper, Ruthless took sides very quickly. He didn't care anything about the artistic merits of the piece. The fact that it was fashioned of pure gold was all he needed to know. He reasoned that he could steal the chalice, melt it down, then sell it, and no one would be the wiser as to where it came from.

The church was illuminated by a bank of flickering candles and dust-laden bars of sun which splashed pools of shimmering light against the walls and onto the floor. It had been a long time since Ruthless had set foot in a church and that had been a nondenominational Protestant church with plain walls and rough-hewn, backless wooden benches. This church, despite its rather plain-looking appearance outside, was beautiful and intimidating inside.

The pews were fine, mahogany pieces with red-upholstered kneelers. The walls were filled with bas-relief carvings of the tortured face of Jesus. These were the Stations of the Cross, though Ruthless had never heard the term and had no idea what he was seeing.

At the front of the church there were several niches filled with statues; the Virgin Mary and other saints whose names Ruthless would have forgotten if he had ever heard them. The most dominating piece, however, was a large cross upon which was affixed a life-size figure of the crucified body of Christ.

The altar table was set with candles and covered with a fine, white linen. And in the middle of the altar table was the thing Ruthless was looking for, the piece that had brought him into the church in the first place. It was a golden cup, beautiful in its simplicity, gleaming softly now because it was caught in a small, precise beam of sunlight. Ruthless cared nothing about its beauty. He saw it only as a piece of gold, and he let out a little grunt of triumph as he picked it up.

"Señor! What are you doing?" a man's voice challenged.

Ruthless looked toward the sound of the voice and saw a large, dark figure emerging from the shadows. The man's right hand was extended and he was holding something, leveled at Ruthless. A pistol!

Ruthless tossed the cup to the side and when it hit the wall, the man in the shadows let out a shout of alarm and turned his attention toward it. With his attention diverted, Ruthless was able to seize the opportunity to draw his own pistol, and he didn't hesitate. He had it out in the blink of an eye and an instant later the walls of the church reverberated with the thunderclap of an exploding shell. The man in the shadows grabbed his chest, then crumpled to the floor. It wasn't until he fell that Ruthless saw it wasn't a gun the man had been holding. It was a cross. He had just shot a priest.

Almost instantly thereafter, the front doors to the church swung open and the men and women of the little village came running in to see what happened.

"It is Padre Sanchez!" someone said in alarm.

"What has happened?"

"He has been shot!"

"You!" someone said, pointing an accusing finger at Ruthless. "You shot a priest! I cannot believe this. What kind of man would shoot a priest?"

"He came toward me," Ruthless explained weakly. "He was holding something in his hand. I...I thought it was a gun."

"You will burn in hell for this," one of the men insisted.

"I thought it was a gun," Ruthless explained. Then he grew angry and, seeing that he was still holding the pistol while none of the villagers appeared to be armed, he pointed his gun at them. "Why do I have to explain anything to you?" he asked. He laughed, cruelly. "I'm the one holding the gun here."

"Shoot me if you wish, Señor," one of the bigger of the men said, starting toward him, menacingly. "But your bullets will not stop me before I kill you with my bare hands."

"Tomas!" the priest gasped, reaching up, weakly, to clutch at the big man who had started toward Ruthless.

"Padre Sanchez, you are alive," Tomas said. "Do not hurt him, Tomas."

"But, Padre," Tomas protested.

"Do not hurt him," Padre Sanchez said again. "I am dying. You will grant a dying man this last wish?"

"Si, Padre. But I cannot accept that he will go

unpunished for this terrible sin."

Padre Sanchez coughed, and blood bubbled from his lips, but he managed to get his breath and speak again.

"Do not worry, Tomas. He will not go unpunished. Just now I have spoken with the souls of the eight men and the one woman he has killed. I know that all the Saints of Heaven and all the demons of hell will see that he knows no peace. Together, we will haunt and torment his soul until the day he dies."

"Stay back, all of you!" Ruthless shouted to the others, cocking his pistol and waving it menacingly. "Stay back!"

Holding them at bay, Ruthless left the church, leaped into his saddle and rode away from the town at a full gallop, leaving the gold chalice lying unclaimed on the church floor.

"...the eight men and the one woman he has killed," the priest had said. It was that statement that caused Ruthless to become so frightened that he could leave the chalice behind. How had the priest known about the woman? That had been long ago, before his life as an outlaw and gunfighter had begun. No one knew or even suspected that he had ever killed a woman and yet, somehow, the priest knew!

"Shut up!" Ruthless suddenly shouted, standing

up so quickly that the chair he had been sitting in fell back with a clatter. He pulled his pistol and shot it into the ceiling. "I'll kill the next man who mentions the word ghost to me!"

All conversation came to a complete halt and the saloon was deathly quiet, except for the measured tick-tock of the Regulator clock that hung on the wall above the hat racks.

"Don't just sit there and stare at me either," Ruthless demanded. "Go back to what you were doing. Talk, play cards, drink. Just don't talk about Lattimore or Chaney."

The silence continued until Ruthless fired another shot into the ceiling.

"I said talk!" he demanded.

His last demand elicited some response, though the conversations were forced and difficult. Nevertheless the oppressive silence had been ended and Ruthless was at least, temporarily, granted the peace of not having to hear tales of ghosts.

Over in one corner of the room a few men had collected some money to persuade one of the bar girls to take Ruthless upstairs.

"I'm afraid of him," the girl pouted.

"Girl, you don't have to be afraid of him," one of the men said. "Without that gun he's just another man, and not much of one at that. I reckon you won't have no trouble handlin' him."

"And we're payin' you double your goin' rate," the other man said.

"You gotta do it," the first man insisted. "Without he gets his mind off all this business goin' on aroun' here, there ain't no one goin' to have any peace."

The girl looked at the money for a long moment, then over at Ruthless Blanton who was still sitting alone, staring morosely into his drink. She sighed, then took the money and stuck it down into the garter of her stocking.

"All right," she said. "I'll do it. But if he tries anything funny, I'm comin' out of there right that minute if I have to come out butt naked."

One of the two men laughed. "Well, that's almost worth waitin' aroun' for to see if it happens," he teased.

The bar girl left Ruthless' two benefactors and walked over to his table. By the time she reached it, she was wearing a practiced smile, and she coughed, lightly, to get his attention.

"Yes?" Ruthless asked, looking up at her. "What do you want?"

"My name is Amy," the girl said.

"All right, so your name is Amy. What do you want, Amy?"

"I just want to make you feel good, that's all."

Ruthless raised his hand to send her away, then he stopped. It had been a while since he had a woman, and this one was a particularly comely girl. And she was offering herself to him. Why not enjoy the opportunity. Maybe the girl was right. Maybe it would make him feel better. He tossed down the rest of his drink, then stood up and reached for her.

"Let's go," he grunted.

Ruthless was awakened by a cock's crow. When he opened his eyes he saw that the sun was shining through the dirty windowpane, illuminating an even dirtier room. Amy lay in bed beside him, snoring softly. She was naked and, in the glare of early morning sunlight, somewhat less attractive than she had seemed to him the night before.

Ruthless sat up without waking her, then reached for his clothes which were on the chair beside the bed. When he was fully dressed a few minutes later he buckled on his gun belt, then slid the gun out from under his pillow and slipped it down into the holster. He walked over to the chest to pour some water from the pitcher into the basin when, through the window, something on the street caught his eye. He returned to the window, but the pane was so dirty that he couldn't be sure of what he was seeing, so he slid the window up for a better look.

"What the hell?" he bellowed, shouting so loudly that Amy sat up in bed.

"What is it?" she asked. "What's wrong?"

"I'll kill him!" Ruthless shouted as he clattered

down the stairs, his pistol in his hand. "I'll kill who-ever did this!"

Ruthless ran out the front door of the Angry Bull, then down the street toward the front of the marshal's office. The object he had seen from the room on the second floor of the Angry Bull was much easier to see now. It was a hearse, the same hearse which had carried Lance Chaney's body to the cemetery.

"Who left this here?" Ruthless shouted into the early morning street. "Who did this?"

Here and there, along the street, curtains were pulled to one side as the citizens of the town, safe now, in their own homes, looked out onto the street to watch the rantings of the man who had come to take control of their town. They saw what Ruthless saw: a hearse with its' team of black horses stand-ing stoically in harness, with a driver dressed all in black, wearing a black stovepipe hat, sitting quietly on the seat.

When Ruthless reached the hearse he looked in through the glass side and saw lying not in, but on top of a coffin, the body of Titus Lattimore.

"Get this hearse out of here!" Ruthless demanded, walking around to the front of the vehicle to speak to the driver. "Do you hear me? Get this hearse... Ahhh!!!" he suddenly shouted. Then, before the shocked view of everyone who had been looking through their windows, Ruthless opened fire on the driver, shooting him again and again until he was out of bullets and the hammer of his pistol fell on empty chambers.

What was even more shocking to the citizens of the town, was the fact that the bullets seemed to have no effect on the driver.

Ruthless turned and ran then. He ran hard and fast all the way back down the street to the Angry Bull. When someone looked in on him a moment later, they saw him at the bar, drinking whiskey straight from a bottle.

A few of the townspeople let their curiosity get control of their fear, and they walked out into the street to get a closer look at the hearse and at the driver who couldn't be stopped by bullets. That was when they saw that the figure on the driver's seat, dressed all in black, was a human skeleton.

CHAPTER 16

"THERE ARE SIX BULLET HOLES IN MR. Albritton's funeral suit," Doc Presnell said to Lance, Buck and Lily.

"Can they be patched up, or are we going to have to buy him a new one?" Buck asked.

Doc Presnell laughed. "Oh, they can be patched up all right," he said. "Besides, Albritton told me he would take care of it himself. He allowed as how he had never laughed as hard in his life as he did while he was watching the ferocious Mr. Ruthless Blanton shooting holes through his suit and my office skeleton."

"How is the skeleton?" Lance asked.

Doc Presnell laughed. "What can you do to a skeleton?" he replied. "Ol' Mr. Bones is far beyond feeling anything, I assure you."

"Lance, I think we've got Ruthless right where

we want him," Buck said. "I think it's time I called the gentleman out."

Lance smiled back at him. "I think you're right, Little Brother," he said. "You can call him out if you want to, but I'm the one who has a score to settle with him, not only for what he did to me, but for what he did to Dan."

"What do you mean?"

"I mean when the showdown comes, I plan to be the one standing in the street, facing him."

"Lance, no!" Lily said.

Buck shook his head. "Can't let you do that, Big Brother," he said. "He's much too fast for you."

"If we play our cards right, fast won't count," Lance said.

"You've got an idea?" Buck asked.

Lance smiled. "Yeah," he said. "And a pretty good one, I think. See what you think of this."

Over the next few hours, many of the outlaws and drifters who had come into Barlow to take advantage of the "open town" Ruthless had declared began to leave. As a few of them observed, they hadn't really gained anything by being here in the first place. They had come hoping for an opportunity to pick up some easy money, but that opportunity never came. And without money there was no fun.

The only advantage at all was that with Ruthless

the marshal and Lattimore the deputy, they weren't likely to be arrested. In truth, however, most of them were outlaws of such minimal importance that the local authorities didn't normally bother them anyway, as long as they behaved themselves while in town.

Two such drifters, whose pockets were emptier now than they had been when they came into town, were saddling their horses as they prepared to leave.

"I don't know, August," one of the drifters said. "Maybe before Lattimore got hisself killed, we could'a come up with some way to make a little money around here. I mean he was a fella you could at least talk to. But with him bein' dead, that leaves us havin' to deal direct with Ruthless Blanton. And you can say what you want to, Ruthless Blanton ain't no easy man to talk to, or even to be aroun' for that matter."

"You ain't tellin' me nothin' I don't already know," Angus replied. "I went up to him a while ago an' tried to tell him there weren't nothin' goin' on aroun' here 'cept some folks havin' a little bit of fun with him, but he wouldn't have none of it."

"I don't know but what I ain't a little spooked myself," Jake admitted. "You got to admit there's some strange things goin' on aroun' here. I mean what with there not bein' a mark on Lattimore's body to tell how he was killed, then him turnin' up in that hearse an' all. An' it bein' driven by a skeleton."

"Oh, hell, Jake, that skeleton don't mean nothin'," Angus assured him. "I seen it the other day when I went into the Doc's office to see if he had a tonic I could take for my stomach."

"You did?"

"Sure, lots of doctors have skeletons in their office. They have to study them all the time. If they didn't know where a person's bones was, they couldn't never do no doctorin' on 'em."

***

"Did you tell Ruthless that the skeleton come from Doc's office?" Jake asked.

"Well, like I say, I figured I would. But when I tried to talk to him real friendly-like, why, he damn near bit my head off," Angus answered. "So as far as I'm concerned the sonofabitch can just stand down at the other end of the bar there an' drink 'til he drops."

"Yeah, that's what I say," Jake agreed. "Come on, let's you an' me get the hell out of here." "You got 'ny idea where to go?" Angus asked, as he swung into his saddle.

"Not really," Jake replied as he, too, mounted his animal. "But I reckon that any place we go is bound to be better'n this place."

It was a little after ten o'clock in the morning when Angus and Jake rode out of town. There had been several who left before them and now no more than two or three of the drifters remained. Those who remained behind did so not out of any sense of loyalty to Ruthless Blanton, but simply because they were by nature men of such low drive and self-esteem that they had not yet developed the initiative to leave.

With the rapid departure of the more undesirable elements, the good citizens of Barlow began to reassert themselves. Stores which had been closed, or had only been opened for reduced hours, began to re-enter the world of commerce. The streets and sidewalks of Barlow were busy, once again, with men and women hurrying to their daily rounds. Construction began again on the new hardware store between Poindexter's Emporium and Bixby's Leathergoods.

Ruthless seemed unaware that everyone had left, unaware even that the townspeople were taking their town back from him, right from under his nose. From the moment he had emptied his gun into the skeleton he had discovered driving the hearse, until nearly noon, he had stood morose and alone at the end of the bar in the Angry Bull.

"How come he ain't drunk?" one of the drifters who had remained behind asked.

"Truth to tell, he ain't doin' that much drinkin'," one of the others answered. "I been watchin' him an' he ain't had no more'n three glasses of whiskey this livelong mornin'."

"Well, what's he doin' if he ain't drinkin'?"

"He's just standin' there, starin'."

"What's he lookin' at?"

"That's just it. He ain't lookin' at nothin', he's just starin'. And he ain't listenin' to nothin' neither. It's most like he ain't even there atall, 'cept you can see him, plain as day."

"I tell you the truth, I don't hold much store by all this ghost business. But seein' Ruthless Blanton just standin' there like that, without lookin' at nobody an' without sayin' nothin'…why, it pure gives me the willies. You never can tell what a fella like that is liable to do. It's most like he could just go mad at any moment an' commence to blazin' away in here."

"Yeah, it's spooky, all right."

The two drifters, who by now were so low of funds that they had to share a beer, sat at a table far enough away from Ruthless Blanton to avoid any accidental contact with him. They were, then, in an excellent position to see the man who suddenly, and unexpectedly, stepped through the front door, carrying a double-barrel shotgun. When the man leveled the shotgun at Ruthless, they cringed back against the wall and waited for the blast.

It didn't come.

"Ruthless Blanton?" the man with the shotgun said.

Ruthless looked up into the twin barrels, almost as if he were disinterested in the fact that, with the slightest twitch of his finger, the man holding the gun could take half his head off.

"Who are you?" Ruthless asked.

"I'm Buck Chaney. I sent you a little note, telling you I was coming. Remember?"

"You didn't show up."

Buck smiled. "Oh, yes, I did. I just didn't want to meet the welcoming committee you sent for me, that's all."

"So. Are you going to kill me now?" Ruthless asked.

"That's what I'm going to do."

"With a shotgun? The bartender over at the Easy Pickin's said you weren't particular about how you killed someone."

Buck smiled. "Oh, I'm not going to use the shotgun," he said. "I just carried it with me to get your attention. Do I have your attention, Mr. Blanton?"

"You've got it," Ruthless answered.

"Good. Now, here's what I want you to do. I'm going to walk down to the other end of the street. At noon, you come out the door, into the street at this end. We'll start toward each other."

"When do we shoot?"

"Oh, you can shoot any time you feel like it," Buck said.

Ruthless chuckled. "You think doin' it that way will even things up for me bein' faster than you? Well, it won't."

"We'll see, Mr. Blanton," Buck said easily. "We'll see."

Buck backed out of the saloon door, then started up to the other end of the street. Ruthless, who had been so silent all morning long, now became quite animated. Here was a tangible enemy, someone who walked and talked, and, more importantly, someone who could be killed.

"Bartender," Ruthless said. "Serve all my friends a drink, on me."

"Yes, sir, Mr. Blanton," the bartender replied. Ruthless looked around the saloon, then frowned, as if noticing for the first time that so many people were gone.

"Where is everyone?" he asked. "Where did everybody go?"

"Oh, they just sort of drifted out, the same way they drifted in," the bartender replied.

"You're still here."

"Yes, sir. I got no other place to go."

"What about you two?" Ruthless asked the two

drifters who had been sharing a beer, but now stepped up to the bar to take advantage of their good fortune. "Why are you still here?"

"We wouldn't want to leave you, Ruthless," one of them said.

"What's your name?" Ruthless asked as he took a drink of his own whiskey.

"I'm Pauley. This here is Bert."

"Well, Pauley, Bert, soon as I kill Mr. Buck Chaney, there's goin' to be some changes around here," Ruthless said.

"Yes, sir," Pauley said, taking an appreciative swallow from his own drink.

"No, I mean it," Ruthless insisted. "I'm goin' to need some new deputies, so I'm appointin' you two. An' the first thing we're goin' to have to do is collect some taxes."

"Collect taxes?" Pauley asked.

"Sure. The good citizens of this town are goin' to have to pay us to protect them, aren't they?" Ruthless suggested.

"Yeah," Pauley said, smiling broadly now that he caught on to what Ruthless was saying. "Yeah, they're goin' to have to pay us."

"Good. I'm glad to see that you understand." Ruthless took his pistol from his holster then and checked the cylinder. It wasn't until that moment that he realized he hadn't reloaded since emptying his gun at the skeleton that morning. He punched the spent cartridges out, then replaced them with fresh ammunition. After that he spun the cylinder, then put the pistol back into his holster.

"Now, deputies," he said. "We wouldn't want anything to happen that might ruin our plans, would we?"

"No," Pauley answered.

"Good, I'm glad you see that. Because I want the two of you to go out the back door, then down the alley about halfway to the other end of the street. Find yourselves a place where you can get a good, open shot at Chaney. When you hear me begin to shoot, you open fire too."

"Right," Pauley said.

"Got you, Ruthless," Bert added. The two men tossed down the rest of their drink, then darted out the back door. Ruthless reached up to square his hat, then he started out the front.

The main street of the town was four blocks long from the Angry Bull Saloon at one end, to the town church at the other. When Ruthless stepped out into the middle of the street he saw Buck Chaney four blocks away, also in the middle of the street. Buck waved at Ruthless and Ruthless waved back. The two men started walking toward each other.

The street, which but moments ago had been busy, was now totally deserted as everyone had hastened to get out of danger. Ruthless knew that the people were watching from behind the corners and from inside the shops and stores. It was good that they were watching, for after they saw him kill Buck Chaney, they would be too frightened to offer any resistance to his intention to tax them for his "services."

There would be a few other changes as well. Ruthless wasn't sure whether there was really a ghost or not, but he had come up with a way to deal with the situation. If he wasn't a ghost, then Ruthless could stop him right away. He planned to kill one citizen of the town, every time the ghost made its appearance. If it was someone trying to play a trick on him, that would turn the tables on them.

On the other hand, if it was a real ghost, then it was obviously here to try and protect the town from him. If the ghost saw that each time he made an appearance it was causing one more town person to lose his life, then even it might be persuaded to cease its hauntings.

There were four cross streets across the main street, and Buck was approaching his first one. He was still too far away for Ruthless to open fire. A wagon came out of the first cross street. The driver drove his team right across the main street, as if he didn't know, or perhaps, didn't care that he had put himself and his team right in the middle of a gunfight.

Ruthless halted until the wagon was gone, then he started walking again. He had taken no more than two steps when he suddenly realized that the man coming toward him wasn't Buck Chaney! It was Lance Chaney!

"What the hell?" Ruthless gasped. He stopped walking and stared incredulously.

The wagon which had just crossed the street came back, again temporarily blocking Ruthless' view of his adversary. When the wagon was gone the second time, he saw Buck Chaney continuing to walk toward him just as he had been.

"What is it?" Ruthless yelled. "What's going on?"

"What's the matter, Blanton?" Buck shouted. "Are you losing your nerve?"

"Who are you?"

"You know who I am. I'm Buck Chaney, the man who is going to kill you."

"No! Before! Your brother was here!"

"Oh, I'm sure he is here," Buck said easily. "He's watching and waiting. And when I get through with you in this life, he's going to take care of you in the next."

Another wagon passed between them.

"Get out of the way!" Ruthless shouted angrily. He pulled his pistol and waved it excitedly at the driver, motioning for him to hurry across the street. "Get that wagon out of my way, you fool!"

When the wagon cleared the street so that Ruthless could see the man coming toward him again he saw that it was, once more, Lance Chaney.

"No!" Ruthless screamed, his voice going nearly falsetto in its terror. He started running toward Lance, shooting wildly, his bullets kicking up dirt just at Lance's feet, then whining off into the distance.

When Pauley and Bert heard the shooting begin, they stepped around the comer of the building where they had been waiting and raised their guns, looking for an opportunity to come to Ruthless' support. They had to wait for the wagon to get out of the way and, because their attention was riveted on the street in front of them, they didn't notice that a man was clinging, doubled over, to the side of the wagon that was away from Ruthless. This was Buck Chaney; and as soon as the wagon was clear of the street, he hopped down. That was when he saw the two men, getting ready to shoot at Lance.

"Do you two men have something in mind?" he asked, leveling his gun toward them.

Pauley and Bert dropped their guns and raised their hands.

In the meantime, out in the street, Ruthless continued his mad run toward Lance, firing with every step. Lance, who had his own pistol out, had assumed the position of a man fighting a duel. He presented his right side to his onrushing adversary.

His right arm and hand were extended straight out from his shoulder, as he took a long and careful aim. Lance wasn't fast, but he was a good shot, and he was extremely cool under pressure.

He squeezed the trigger.

The Easy Pickin's was the place to be that evening. The entire town showed up to celebrate. When someone said that it seemed a little odd to be celebrating Ruthless Blanton getting himself killed, he was told that they weren't celebrating Ruthless' death, they were celebrating Lance's resurrection. Lily bought a round of drinks for everyone, then Poindexter bought, then Bixby.

Lance and Buck weren't the only ones being feted, however. Doc came in for a lot of praise for his quick thinking in declaring Lance dead in the first place. Jenny and Sam Goodbody were saluted for their part in maintaining the charade, and George Toomey wasn't left out. Even Mr. Albritton, whose somber profession and need to constantly maintain a proper decorum normally kept him away from such activity, was toasted several times. By the time that dignified gentleman left the saloon to tend to the final remains of the late Ruthless Blanton, he was having a difficult time walking a straight line.

"And now, if I could please have your attention?" Mayor Cravens said, climbing up onto one of the tables. "People, please, could I have your attention?"

"Lord, wouldn't you know it? Give a politician a crowd and he'll make a speech every time," someone said, and the others laughed.

"Please," Mayor Cravens said, holding up his hands for quiet. "I have an announcement to make."

The part-time mayor and full-time newspaper editor finally managed to quiet the crowd, then he cleared his throat for the announcement he wanted to make.

"The city council has just held a meeting, and we have selected a new town marshal. Folks, it gives me great pleasure to offer the title and the pay, as well as the job, to the man who has been acting as our marshal...even from the grave..."

The others laughed.

"Lance Chaney."

There was a round of applause.

"What do you say, Lance? Will you take the job?"

"Of course he will," someone shouted, and several others added their own encouragement.

Finally Lance, under everyone's urging, stood up to say a few words of his own.

"As you know," he said, "I was offered this job once before, but I turned it down because I didn't feel I was qualified. As a result, we went out and found another man...a very good man, in Dan Efrem."

"Here, here," someone said.

"And now, Dan Efrem is dead," Lance said quietly. "In a way, I can't help but think it was, somehow, my fault. If I had taken the job when it was offered the first time, instead of letting another man do it for me, that good man would be alive today. I don't intend to let another good man die because I refused the job, so I'll take it, but I'm going to need an edge."

"What kind of edge?"

"The Chaney edge," Lance said, smiling broadly. He looked over at Buck. "I need you as my deputy, Buck. How about it?"

"Yeah, Buck, how about it?" someone in the crowd asked.

"Lance, you know I've…"

"Got another town to see, another hole-card to draw to, and another bar girl to spark," Lance completed for him. "Yeah, I know. That's why I'm going to hire someone else as my town deputy. You are going to be my traveling deputy."

"Traveling deputy? What's that?"

"A traveling deputy is someone who is free to go anywhere he wants, anytime he wants. I just want you to come back whenever I need you."

"That's all you want?"

"That's all I want."

"Buck," Jenny said, smiling seductively. "I don't know anything about seeing another town, or playing in another card game, but if it's girls you're wanting to spark, why, I think we could keep you busy enough right here." She pointed to the other bar girls who, like Jenny, smiled sweetly and invitingly at him. The men whooped and laughed at the invitation.

"Buck Chaney, if you turn down an offer like that, you are nowhere near the gentleman I always imagined you to be, and I am going to be very disappointed," Lily said sternly.

Buck laughed, then held his hands up in surrender. "I've been accused of many things," he said. "But I've never been accused of disappointing a lady." He stuck his hand out to grab his brother's. "Lance," he added. "You've got the Chaney edge."

A LOOK AT BOOK 3: THE HUNTERS

A STORY OF GOOD VERSUS EVIL…

When Lance Chaney's ex-commanding officer from the Civil War comes to him for help, the Barlow Marshal cannot refuse, even when things don't add up.

With his brother Buck riding alongside him, the pair find more trouble than they care to. From Indians, to outlaws, their trail is dotted with violence.

Meanwhile back in Barlow, Lance's remaining deputy is killed, leaving the town wide open for the lawless. But out of the freezing winter comes a one-eyed man who seems to be fit for the job.

Except Ben Travers has a plan. He and his gang are going to take Barlow for all it has, and he doesn't care how many corpses he has to walk over to get it.

Best-selling western author Robert Vaughan keeps you glued to your seat with the third Chaney Brothers Western.

AVAILABLE NOW

ABOUT THE AUTHOR

Robert Vaughan sold his first book when he was 19. That was 57 years and nearly 500 books ago. Vaughan wrote, produced, and appeared in the History Channel documentary Vietnam Homecoming. His books have hit the NYT bestseller list seven times. He has won the Spur Award, the PORGIE Award (Best Paperback Original), the Western Fictioneers Lifetime Achievement Award, received the Readwest President's Award for Excellence in Western Fiction, is a member of the American Writers Hall of Fame and is a Pulitzer Prize nominee. Vaughn is also a retired army officer, helicopter pilot with three tours in Vietnam. And received the Distinguished Flying Cross, the Purple Heart, The Bronze Star with three oak leaf clusters, the Air Medal for valor with 35 oak leaf clusters, the Army Commendation Medal, the Meritorious Service Medal, and the Vietnamese Cross of Gallantry.